Welcome to the Secret World of Alex Mack!

I was really psyched when I was chosen to represent my school in the local Junior Olympics. But what if the race is another trap set by the plant to find the GC-161 kid? Besides, thanks to Annie's "experiments" on my powers, I'm supercharged with excess energy! It's going to be hard to blend in (let alone run a race) while I'm glowing like a neon light and attracting all the trash in Paradise Valley. So much for the thrill of victory. Let me explain. . . .

I'm Alex Mack. I was just another average kid until my first day of junior high.

One minute I'm walking home from school—the next there's a *crash!* A truck from the Paradise Valley Chemical plant overturns in front of me, and I'm drenched in some weird chemical.

And since then—well, nothing's been the same. I can move objects with my mind, shoot electrical charges through my fingertips, and morph into a liquid shape . . . which is handy when I get in a tight spot!

My best friend, Ray, thinks it's cool—and my sister Annie thinks I'm a science project.

They're the only two people who know about my new powers. I can't let anyone else find out—not even my parents—because I know the chemical plant wants to find me and turn me into some experiment.

But you know something? I guess I'm not so average anymore!

The Secret World of Alex Mack™

Available from MINSTREL Books

For orders other than by individual consumers, Pocket Books grants a discount on the purchase of **10 or more** copies of single titles for special markets or premium use. For further details, please write to the Vice-President of Special Markets, Pocket Books, 1633 Broadway, New York, NY 10019-6785, 8th Floor.

For information on how individual consumers can place orders, please write to Mail Order Department, Simon & Schuster Inc., 200 Old Tappan Road, Old Tappan, NJ 07675.

NICKELODEON®

the secret world of

ALEX MACK™

Go for the Gold!

Diana G. Gallagher

A MINSTREL® BOOK

Published by POCKET BOOKS
New York   London   Toronto   Sydney   Tokyo   Singapore

The sale of this book without its cover is unauthorized. If you purchased this book without a cover, you should be aware that it was reported to the publisher as "unsold and destroyed." Neither the author nor the publisher has received payment for the sale of this "stripped book."

This book is a work of fiction. Names, characters, places and incidents are products of the author's imagination or are used fictitiously. Any resemblance to actual events or locales or persons, living or dead, is entirely coincidental.

A MINSTREL PAPERBACK *Original*

 A Minstrel Book published by
POCKET BOOKS, a division of Simon & Schuster Inc.
1230 Avenue of the Americas, New York, NY 10020

Copyright © 1996 by Viacom International Inc., and RHI Entertainment, Inc. All rights reserved. Based on the Nickelodeon series entitled "The Secret World of Alex Mack."

All rights reserved, including the right to reproduce this book or portions thereof in any form whatsoever. For information address Pocket Books, 1230 Avenue of the Americas, New York, NY 10020

ISBN: 0-671-55862-5

First Minstrel Books printing August 1996

10 9 8 7 6 5 4 3 2 1

NICKELODEON and all related titles, logos and characters are trademarks of Viacom International, Inc.

A MINSTREL BOOK and colophon are registered trademarks of Simon & Schuster Inc.

Cover photography by Blake Little and Danny Feld

Printed in the U.S.A.

For Annie Peifer,
with affection and gratitude
for her gracious help

Go for the Gold!

CHAPTER 1

Usually, Alex enjoyed hanging out in the garage with Annie, helping her sister with her scientific experiments. It was just about the only time they spent together. However, at high noon on a sizzling summer day, the garage felt like a gigantic oven. Sitting on a chair watching spider webs fry on the ceiling was trying Alex's patience. Sighing, she shifted position.

"Hold still, Alex!" Annie ordered.

"Give me a break, Annie," Alex retorted. "This seat is hard, and I've been sitting here forever."

"You've been sitting here for exactly"—Annie checked her watch—"twenty minutes and thirty-two seconds."

"Well, it seems longer," Alex complained. Her tank top stuck to her sweaty skin and her scalp itched under the close-fitting helmet on her head. "It's sweltering in here. Can't we at least open the window?"

"Alex, you know better." Annie shook her head. "All we need is some nosy neighbor spotting us and asking questions. I can't very well say that I'm building a device to regulate and monitor the electrical energies stored in my little sister, the human battery."

Annie had a point, Alex conceded silently as she stuck her hand under the helmet to sneak a scratch. Constructed of curved metal strips, the helmet was covered with electrodes connected by a tangle of different colored wires. Cables ran from the helmet to a control panel on the work bench, which Annie fiddled with every now and then.

"Everyone knows you're a scientific wizard," Alex said to her older sister. "If anyone asks, just tell them this thing measures brain waves or something."

"The only security is total security," Annie insisted. "The window will have to stay closed."

Annie wasn't going to budge, and Alex was too hot to argue. Except for Annie and Raymond

Alvarado, her best friend and next door neighbor, no one knew about her very unusual abilities. Secrecy was essential if Alex wanted to continue living as a typical teenager.

Of course, Alex thought as Annie made an adjustment on the helmet, *having the crazy powers I have is hardly typical. And having a sister who wants to win the Nobel Prize for scientific achievement doesn't make things any easier. Even when she's trying to help, like now.*

"So what is this gizmo supposed to do again?" Alex asked.

"We're charting the amount of electrical energy your body stores under normal circumstances—normal for you, that is. I need to know if there's a limit to the voltage you can tolerate. We don't know if your electrical storage capacity is potentially dangerous to you or not."

"Dangerous! In what way?" Alex frowned. So far, the only danger Alex faced because of her powers was being identified by Danielle Atron. If Ms. Atron, the chief executive officer of Paradise Valley Chemical, found out Alex was the kid who had been drenched with GC-161, Alex would become a full-time experiment in the chemical plant's lab rather than Annie's part-time science project. That was a big enough

3

threat to deal with, but now Annie had to come up with another one.

"For one thing, we don't know if you can get overcharged," Annie explained. "And if you can, what would an electrical overload do to you?"

Alex shuddered, remembering what had happened to their father's old computer during a thunderstorm power outage when she was six. George Mack didn't have a surge protector back then, and the computer had short-circuited when the electricity came back on.

"You mean I could fry my brain?" Alex asked, her eyes growing larger.

"I think that's a pretty remote possibility, but we have to consider everything," Annie said as she connected a wire to a control panel on the workbench. She then stepped back and said to her sister, "Zap something."

Alex extended her hand to turn on an old radio on a step stool nearby, then quickly drew it back. She eyed her sister and said, "What if this hat gadget of yours short-circuits?"

"It won't," Annie said impatiently. "Trust me."

Reluctantly, Alex squinted in concentration and pointed to the radio without touching it. She zapped an electrical bolt into the radio and one of her mom's favorite golden oldies came blaring through the small speaker. Alex adjusted the knob with a thought, tuning into her favorite rock station, then turned up the volume. In her opinion, moving things telekinetically with her mind was the most useful of her powers.

"Alex!"

"What?" Alex blinked innocently.

"You're skewing my data. Just zap, okay?"

Alex nodded and zapped the radio off.

Frowning thoughtfully, Annie checked the panel, then wiggled a wire on the helmet. Then she just stood with her arms folded in front of her and stared at the panel again.

"Come *on*, Annie. If I stay in this inferno much longer, I'm going to *melt*."

"Don't you dare!"

"That was just a figure of speech, Annie. I didn't mean for real." Alex grinned. Nobody else in the whole world could threaten to melt and mean it. Being able to turn into a silvery puddle of ooze at will was the most bizarre side effect of GC-161.

"Oh. Well, okay," Annie said absently. Shrugging, Annie began to fiddle with the helmet again. "Nothing registered on my monitor. There must be a loose connection. Just give me a few more minutes—"

"Alex!"

Both girls jumped at the sound of their mother's voice.

"Just a minute, Mom!" Annie threw up her hands in exasperation and looked at Alex. "I thought she went to the store."

"She must have just gotten back," Alex whispered.

"Are you in there?" Barbara Mack called out.

Alex looked at the door, where she heard her mother's voice, and gasped as the doorknob started to turn. Thinking quickly, she instantly projected an electromagnetic force field to keep the door closed. Barbara and George Mack were totally unaware of their youngest daughter's unique powers, and keeping the secret from them was a constant challenge. *One of these days they're going to find out*, Alex thought. *Especially if Annie keeps forgetting to lock the garage door.*

"Get this thing off me, Annie!" Alex whispered.

Annie quickly removed the helmet and shoved it into a box under the workbench. Then she dashed to the door and opened it.

"Annie, you've got to stop locking this door,"

Mrs. Mack said sternly. "It's very annoying when I need to get something in here. I'm not going to steal your scientific secrets and sell them to the highest bidder."

"Sorry, Mom."

Fanning herself with her hand, Mrs. Mack frowned. "It's like an oven in here. I'm surprised you two haven't baked to a crisp."

"You wanted me?" Alex asked her mother hopefully. Right now, doing a brutally boring chore would be infinitely better than staying in the garage with Annie. *At least the house is air-conditioned,* Alex thought as she pushed her long light brown hair off her damp forehead.

"Nicole and Robyn are here, Alex," Mrs. Mack said.

"Thanks, Mom. Later, Annie." *Much later,* Alex thought as she bolted from the garage into the kitchen.

"Hey, Robyn! I thought your family was on vacation at"—Alex burst into the living room and stopped short—"the lake," she finished.

Nicole Wilson and Robyn Russo were sitting on the couch, and a girl Alex had never seen before sat between them. She was small and trim, with close-cropped, curly dark hair, emerald green eyes, and a gorgeous, golden tan. They

7

were all wearing brightly colored tank tops and running shorts. The three girls looked up at Alex expectantly.

"We had to come back early," Robyn said, scratching her shoulder. Robyn was a redhead, and her pale skin was peeling from too much sun. An explosion of freckles on her face looked like a blotchy tan splattered over sunburned red.

"My parents decided to have a romantic midnight picnic in the woods and got poison ivy," Robyn went on. "I'll spare you the embarrassing details," she said, rolling her eyes.

Nicole's dark eyes sparkled mischievously as she confided to her new friend, "Disaster runs in Robyn's family. She lives on the brink of certain doom."

"No, I'm just realistic," Robyn insisted. Flipping her long hair back, Robyn fixed the new girl with a serious gaze. "At least, I'm always prepared for the worst. Nicole just jumps into her current cause of the week and figures she's going to come out on top because she's on the side of truth, justice, and the American way."

"And I always do." Nicole's dark hair bounced as she nodded.

The new girl looked slightly bewildered as she glanced back and forth between Robyn and Nicole. Then, with a shy smile, she looked at Alex and shrugged.

"Hi. I'm Alex Mack." Smiling, Alex extended her hand.

"Oh, gosh! Sorry, Alex," Nicole said. "This is Jackie Addison. She just moved in on my street."

"Glad to meet you, Alex," Jackie said, shaking her hand.

"Same here." There wasn't room on the couch for a fourth, so Alex sank into an armchair. "I'm glad you all stopped by. I've been going nuts with nothing to do."

"We can't stay." Nicole jumped to her feet.

"Why not?" Alex asked.

"Because tryouts for the junior-high Olympic team are this afternoon," Nicole said. "The announcement was in the chemical plant newsletter. Aren't you going over?"

Alex stared at her friends in surprise. She hadn't realized they planned to try out. Her father had mentioned Paradise Valley Chemical was sponsoring the event, an Olympic-like competition for junior high schools in the county. But Alex hadn't considered trying out because it was too dangerous. Although Danielle Atron often sponsored community events designed to boost her image, sometimes those events were

nothing but schemes to trap the GC-161 kid—
Alex. The risk of being discovered was just too
great for Alex to take unnecessary chances.

"When did you decide to do this?" Alex was
genuinely curious. Nicole rejected organized
sports because, as she put it, she didn't want to
be a glorified modern gladiator. Alex thought it
was quite possible that Nicole could find something politically incorrect about baking apple pie.
And since almost failing the Rooney Runabout
in gym class—an obstacle course the students
had to run through last year—Robyn had decided never to get involved with strenuous
sports again.

"Trying out was Jackie's idea," Nicole said.

"Well, actually it was my dad's idea," Jackie
said. "He just started working at Paradise Valley
Chemical and he's trying to make a good impres-
sion on the boss. I guess he wants to show Danielle Atron that the Addisons are team players
and solid citizens, you know?"

"Yeah, I guess I do," Alex said with a knowing
nod. Her parents always encouraged her to par-
ticipate in such activities, but she could never
explain to them why she avoided the events.
They didn't know about GC-161 or Danielle
Atron's determination to find her. Neither did

her girlfriends, so Alex wasn't quite sure what to say to them just now.

"I've never been interested in sports, and I really didn't want to try out," Jackie continued, "but my dad seemed so disappointed when he found that out. He went to college on a track-and-field scholarship." Jackie sighed. "Then I decided it might be a good way to meet some of the kids before school starts, so I agreed to give it a shot."

"It can't hurt to try," Alex said. She understood Jackie's desire to please her father. Alex's father was a brilliant scientist. Unlike Annie, Alex had to struggle to get Bs in science and math. Her dad never said so, but sometimes she wondered if her lack of scientific aptitude bothered him.

Alex raised an eyebrow as Nicole stood up, stretched her arms over her head, and touched her toes. "It's for a good cause," Nicole explained defensively. "The money from ticket sales will be donated to the Special Olympics."

"I didn't know that," Alex said. "What events are you trying out for?"

"There are just two categories, gymnastics and track." Nicole glanced down at her short form.

"I'm not built for speed, but I do okay on the balance beam."

"*I'm* not trying out for anything," Robyn said. "They're only picking two girls and two boys from each of the three grades, so there's not much point. I wouldn't even make it as an alternate."

"An alternate?" Alex asked.

"Yeah. Like understudies in a play," Nicole said. "An extra girl and boy for track and an extra girl and boy for gymnastics in each grade will be training with the regular team. The alternates will fill in if someone gets sick or something."

"Let me get this straight," Alex said. "There are twelve kids on the regular team: three girls in gymnastics and three boys in gymnastics, three girls in track and three boys in track."

"Right, and a backup team of twelve alternates just in case something goes wrong," Robyn said. "And something always does, you know. Murphy's Law. But they're using kids as coaches and stuff, too, and I think I'd make a good student manager. I have to do something to contribute."

"Yeah." Alex smiled tightly, trying to muster a measure of enthusiasm. With only two positions available, her own chances of making the team weren't that great. She had never really been into gymnastics, and at least a half-dozen girls in their class could outrun her. Some of them were bound to show up. Plus, Jackie would be trying out, and she might have inherited her father's talent for track without knowing it.

"I have a knack for organization," Robyn explained for Jackie's benefit.

"They say everybody's really good at something." Jackie grinned. "I've got a green thumb, which has saved all my mom's houseplants from certain death, but it won't help me run faster."

Alex chewed her lip. She was careful about competing in things where her powers might get her in trouble. But her friends seemed into it, and she didn't want to be the only one not getting involved.

"If we don't get moving soon, we're going to be late," Nicole urged. "We've got to be at the high school stadium by one o'clock. Raymond must be there by now."

"Ray? He's trying out, too?" Alex asked.

"We saw him leaving his house when we got here," Robyn said.

"Go get changed, Alex." Nicole was down on the floor, stretching her hamstrings.

"Me? I don't know if I'm good enough to make the team."

"Of course you are," Robyn said.

"It'll be fun, Alex." Jackie bubbled with enthusiasm.

Right, Alex thought as she trudged upstairs to change. Making a fool of herself was not her idea of fun. And there was always the chance she'd start glowing at the wrong time—which is what happened the last time she raced. But spending the next two weeks alone while her friends were busy getting ready for the county junior high Olympics wouldn't be much fun, either.

Not to mention that the Olympic event might be one of Danielle Atron's traps. Annie certainly wouldn't approve of her trying out. Alex might be setting herself up to get caught.

However, the only alternative was to sit in the hot garage letting Annie poke and prod her while everyone else was having a good time.

Sometimes there was just no way to win.

CHAPTER 2

By the time the girls reached the high school grounds, Alex felt better, in spite of her doubts about her decision to try out. Her friends' excitement was contagious.

"Why do we have to compete as eighth graders?" Nicole wondered aloud. "We all move up to ninth grade this fall. Shouldn't that make us ninth graders now?"

"Technically, yes," Robyn said. "But then Scott wouldn't be eligible for the team."

"Who's he?" Jackie asked as she slowed her jogging pace to stay abreast of the other three girls.

"One of Danielle Atron Junior High's best athletes," Alex explained. "Only he'll be a high school athlete in the fall." Alex stared at the large school building alongside the outdoor stadium just ahead. She tried not to think about Scott being on a different campus from hers. It would be weird not seeing him.

"Scott is unbelievably nice for a cute guy who's smart and a great athlete, too," Robyn said.

"And he'll be hard to beat in gymnastics or track," Nicole added as she led the way along a path beside a high, chain link fence toward the main gate of the sports complex.

"That's the truth," Nicole agreed. "Danielle Atron may be sponsoring the event for all the junior highs in the county, but you can bet she wants her namesake school to win the trophy."

"And we'll have a much better chance if Scott's competing," Alex added.

Jackie frowned as she jogged around a huge tree. "So Ms. Atron set up the rules to make sure Scott could compete. That's why we're all going by last year's grade. I get it, but isn't that like fixing things to give our school an extra advantage?"

"The rules are the same for everyone," Nicole said. "And if that just happens to work in Danielle Atron's favor, no one is going to challenge her. The CEO of Paradise Valley Chemical has the last word on everything around here."

"And she hates to lose," Robyn said. "Especially when she's the one donating the trophy and the medals."

"What medals?" Jackie asked.

"Real gold, silver, and bronze medals for the individual winners," Robyn explained. "Just like in the regular Olympics. Of course, only kids who make the team have a chance to win one."

"I don't care about the medals," Nicole said sincerely. "If I don't make the team cut, I'll spot the other gymnasts or roll out tumbling mats. As long as the profits from what I'm doing will help physically and mentally challenged kids train for the next Special Olympics, I'll be happy."

"You're right, of course, but—" Jackie jogged ahead, then back again. "It would be so cool to have a gold medal framed and hanging on the wall next to my father's awards."

Alex grinned. Everything was right with the world. Robyn was still her same old fatalistic, doom-and-gloom self, and Nicole was fighting for a good cause. Plus they had a nice new friend—who seemed to be in constant motion.

"Aren't you tired?" Alex asked Jackie,

amazed. Jackie had jogged the entire route and still didn't show any signs of wearing down.

"Nope. Just warming up," Jackie said.

When Alex got closer to the stadium and saw the large number of kids waiting for someone to open the main gate, she realized there would be a lot of competition for the Olympic event. She also realized at that moment how much she wanted to make the team. She wanted to know what it would be like to win a real gold medal, to make herself stand out as someone special, to be proud of something she'd worked really hard at, and to make her parents proud, too. Alex forced a smile as they made their way to the edge of the crowd. She was determined not to let the competition discourage her.

"Wow!" Jackie exclaimed. "What a turnout."

"This is great!" Nicole beamed.

"What is, Nicole?" Tossing her dark hair aside, Kelly Phillips looked back at Nicole. Kelly was a year ahead of Alex. She hung out often with Scott, though they weren't officially going together.

"This crowd." Nicole grinned. "If the whole county supports the event like this, we'll raise a bundle for the Special Olympics from ticket sales."

"That's why I'm here," Kelly said. "I can't fit sports into my schedule during school, but it's summer vacation and this is such an important cause." Kelly looked at the brown-haired girl beside her. "Isn't it, Ellen?"

"Sure. Almost as important as winning." Ellen's grin faded as she glanced back. "What are you doing here, Alex?"

"Trying out. Just like you." Alex matched Ellen's intent stare with a steady gaze. Ellen was a super athlete and had been Jessica's best friend before she moved out of town. Jessica was Scott's old girlfriend.

"Everybody's got a reason for trying out, I guess," Ellen went on. "I'm doing it to get in shape, so I can be better than everyone on the track team this fall when school starts."

"Winning isn't everything," Jackie said softly.

Ellen looked as though she couldn't believe what she'd just heard. She exchanged a glance with Kelly, who gave Jackie a curious once-over, and said, "Who are you? I don't believe we've met."

"Jackie just moved to Paradise Valley," Alex said.

"Well, there's something you should know, Jackie." Ellen leaned toward the smaller girl.

"Beating Greenfield and winning the school trophy for Atron *is* what counts here."

"That is *not* what counts in the Olympics," Nicole interrupted. "The modern Olympics were started to promote good sportsmanship and co-operation between the nations of the world."

"In an atmosphere of *friendly* competition," Robyn added.

"Of course," Kelly said coolly. "I'm sure Ellen didn't mean to imply anything different. It's just that the rivalry between Atron and Greenfield is an old and honored tradition, too. It might even boost ticket sales."

"I hate to admit it," Nicole said, "but Kelly's got a point. The school rivalry could be a big draw, and the whole purpose of this competition is to raise money for the Special Olympics."

"I suppose," Alex said. "But putting too much emphasis on winning just doesn't seem right somehow." *Although I wouldn't mind taking home a gold medal*, Alex thought wistfully.

Ellen stiffened. "Good athletes care about being the best, Alex. With your attitude you won't make the team anyway. Why bother trying out?"

"I didn't say I didn't care," Alex protested. "I just—"

"We understand, Alex," Kelly said in her know-it-all tone of voice. "The competition is a lot of pressure, but as Jackie said, winning isn't everything. And being on the team isn't, either. If you don't make the cut, at least you'll know you gave it your best shot, right?" Motioning to Ellen, Kelly turned and eased back into the crowd.

Alex fumed. As usual, Kelly's sugar-coated words disguised her real intent. Without actually saying so, Kelly had just told Alex that she expected her to fail. It was infuriating, especially since almost everyone else seemed unaware of how insulting Kelly could be behind her fake smiles. Including Scott. He seemed to think Kelly was great, and Alex just couldn't understand why.

"Did Kelly just zing you, Alex?" Jackie asked with a bewildered frown.

"It's hard to tell, isn't it?" Alex sighed, then spotted Scott sitting on a bench with some friends. He waved Kelly and Ellen over.

"Alex and Scott are friends." Nicole gestured toward the bench. "And Kelly is dating Scott. So she thinks Alex is competition."

Jackie studied Scott a moment, then nodded in approval. "Kelly must think you're pretty serious competition, Alex. That's why she was nasty to you just now. She's probably threatened by you."

"I doubt it." Alex shrugged. "Anyway, Scott dates Kelly, not me."

"Why is it that all the nice ones are taken?" Robyn frowned, pondering the perplexing question.

"So what's Ellen's excuse?" Jackie asked.

Alex shrugged and grinned. "Ray and I beat her and another star player in one-on-one basketball once."

"Well, that explains it." Jackie laughed.

"Gate's opening." Nicole walked faster.

Two lines began to form as kids surged toward the gate. Alex and her friends moved to the side to avoid the crush. Nicole grabbed Alex and pulled her close so she wouldn't get trampled. Just then Alex felt someone leaning against her. She turned around to see that Jackie was being pushed by Kelly, who was behind her.

Alex gasped as Jackie stumbled and cried out in surprise. Jackie's foot slipped off the edge of the sidewalk and her ankle buckled. Alex quickly grabbed the girl's arm to keep her from falling.

"Sorry," Kelly called back as she and Ellen were swept toward the gate.

"Sure you are." Nicole cast a harsh glance at the two older girls, but they didn't look back.

"I don't think she did it on purpose," Jackie said. She winced as she stepped back onto the concrete. "Did she?"

"Who knows?" Nicole shrugged.

"Are you okay, Jackie?" Alex asked anxiously.

"Yeah, I think so."

"Is it broken or sprained?" Robyn asked.

"No," Jackie said, moving her foot to prove it. "I just turned my ankle a little."

"If that had been me, my ankle would be broken." Robyn nodded with absolute certainly. "In three places."

"Jackie can't run her best on a twisted ankle," Nicole said, looking concerned.

"I'm sure it'll be fine in a few minutes." Smiling, Jackie hobbled as they moved forward. "See? It's better already."

Alex hoped Jackie's diagnosis about her ankle was right. What with Ellen's open hostility, Kelly's condescending attitude, and Jackie's injury, the tryouts were not getting off to a great start.

CHAPTER 3

"Kelly reminds me of a girl at my old school," Jackie said as they headed toward the bleachers.

"In what way?" Alex asked.

"This girl acted nice, but she really wasn't," Jackie said. "I just stayed out of her way."

Robyn nodded. "There's a rotten apple in every barrel."

"It's an unwritten law of the universe," Nicole said.

Jackie laughed, and Alex was impressed with her insight. Most people were taken in by Kelly's charm and didn't realize she only cared about herself.

"Listen up, everybody!" Raymond Alvarado

blew a whistle on a cord around his neck. "Seventh grade! Section four!"

"Who put Ray in charge?" Nicole asked.

"Beats me." Alex shrugged.

"Eight grade! Section five! Ninth—hey! Alex!" Waving, Raymond hurried over. "Glad to see ya! I tried to call you earlier, but the machine picked up."

"Mom was out and I was in the garage with Annie. Guess we didn't hear the phone."

"I'm glad you're trying out," Raymond said. "I didn't expect to see you here."

"I didn't expect to see you either," Alex said.

"What exactly is your function here, Ray?" Robyn asked. "I thought you were going out for the team."

"Mr. Hokaido needed an eighth-grade student coach, so I volunteered. See, I figure athletes get old fast and have to retire early. But coaches don't."

"Unless they have too many losing seasons," Nicole said.

"Is a coach the same as a student manager?" Alex said, knowing that Robyn would want to ask that question since she was hoping to be a student manager.

"No. Louis wanted to be a student manager,

but he won't be back from vacation for two weeks. I don't think they've found anyone else."

Robyn perked up when she heard that. "Great! Who do I see about getting the job?"

"Mr. Hokaido, I guess." Raymond pointed toward the dugout area, where two teachers stood. "Or Ms. Clark." Mr. Hokaido, the earth science teacher who coached gymnastics for girls and boys, was supervising the junior high county Olympics along with Ms. Clark. A junior high history teacher who also coached track, Ms. Clark was lean and strong from running marathons, and she stood a full head taller than Mr. Hokaido.

Robyn was gone in a flash, although Alex didn't see any need for the rush. No one else was at the dugout asking for the job. Everyone was in the bleachers, hoping to be chosen for the team.

After introducing Jackie and Raymond to each other, Alex, Nicole, and Jackie went to join their classmates at the bleachers, sitting down on the bottom row to wait. After the track tryouts, they would all move inside for the gymnastics competition. Alex was certain Nicole had the gymnastic tryouts in the bag. About twenty eighth-grade boys had shown up, but very few girls.

Out on the field, Raymond glanced at his clipboard, then shouted. "Jackie Addison!"

"First?" Jackie paled. "I have to go first?"

"The dreaded alphabetical-order syndrome. I'm always last." Nicole frowned suddenly. "How's your ankle, Jackie?"

Jackie stood up and put her weight on it. "Actually, it's not nearly as sore as it was."

"I can get Raymond to make an exception and put you last," Alex said earnestly. She suspected that Jackie was too timid to ask for special consideration, especially since she was new. "Ray is cool. I'm sure he wants everybody to get a fair chance."

"Addison!" Raymond hollered again. "Front and center!"

"I'll be fine," Jackie said. "Wish me luck."

Jackie didn't seem to be limping as she hurried toward the starting line, Alex noticed. Raymond gave the new girl a hearty thumbs up as she positioned herself for the broad jump. After her jump was measured, she would be timed at the fifty-yard dash, then the hurdles.

Alex held her breath as Jackie ran and took a flying jump. She looked fast and strong, and her form was good. But when she landed, her ankle buckled. Jackie took a short step backward to steady herself; this meant she would lose ten inches off the length of her jump. Alex groaned in disappointment. Jackie was clearly a talented athlete, but luck wasn't with her today.

"Rats," Nicole muttered. "She came so close."

"I knew her ankle was still hurting." Alex crossed her fingers as Jackie dropped into a crouch for the sprint. Ms. Clark fired the starting gun and Raymond clicked his stopwatch as Jackie took off with a dazzling burst of speed.

Alex stood up and cheered and Nicole whistled shrilly. But the two girls grabbed each other as they saw Jackie stumble. "Oh no!" Alex said. "Not again."

Jackie recovered quickly and kept going, but Alex could tell the ankle was holding her back. When Jackie finished the sprint, Alex could see by the expression on her face that she was disappointed with her performance. She was a little wobbly when she started the hurdles course, but still, she cleared all the hurdles without falling.

Raymond made a notation on his clipboard, then called the next girl.

Jackie jogged up and paused to catch her breath. "Sorry I didn't do better, guys, but my ankle just gave out."

"Tough luck, Jackie," a voice behind Alex said.

Alex looked over her shoulder. Kelly was standing on the seat just above them.

"But don't feel bad," Kelly went on. "Some people just don't have the strength for competitive sports. I'm sure there are other things you do really well."

"Jackie stumbled because she twisted her ankle," Nicole said bluntly. "When *you* pushed her."

"Really? How awful!" Kelly's eyes widened with surprise and regret. "I'm so sorry."

Alex doubted that Kelly was truly sorry. Kelly didn't look terribly worried; she seemed to be more concerned with waving to Scott at the moment. Turning around to give Jackie some consoling words, Alex saw that Jackie's eyes were filling with tears.

"Jackie—" Alex said as the new girl took off, hiding her face in her hands. "Jackie!" She kept running and disappeared into the break between bleachers.

"Did I say something to upset her?" Kelly asked, frowning.

"Jackie really wanted to make the team," Alex said. "It was important to her."

"What a shame." Shaking her head, Kelly returned to her seat.

Kelly can be so thoughtless sometimes, Alex thought. With a sigh, she said to Nicole, "I'll go see if Jackie's okay."

"No, I'll go," Nicole said. "You have to be here when Ray calls your name or you'll be out of the competition before it even starts."

Alex's own tension mounted as the other eighth-grade girls took their turns on the course. Everyone seemed to be a little off. Tracy Evans's jump was long, but she fell forward onto her hands when she landed. The next girl knocked down two of the six hurdles. Girl after girl failed to complete the three events without making a major mistake.

What makes me think I can do any better? Alex fretted. When she had helped Robyn train for the Rooney Runabout in gym class, she had managed to get through the course okay, but there hadn't been any pressure on her. This was different.

Then Raymond called her name.

The nervousness Alex had been trying to control suddenly turned to cold fear. Her legs shook and her feet felt like lead weights as she started onto the field.

"Come on, Alex!" Raymond called to hurry her. "Let's go!"

Alex trudged, her cheeks burning with the flush of acute anxiety. One of the more troublesome side effects of the GC-161 compound was Alex's tendency to glow with a golden light whenever she got nervous, which she was at this very moment. Heart pounding against her ribs, she felt breathless and faint when she reached the starting line.

Eyes widening, Raymond waved Ms. Clark back and whispered loudly in Alex's ear, "You're glowing like you did last time!"

"I know."

Raymond gripped her shoulder and looked her in the eye. "I've heard of a natural glow, Alex, but you're overdoing it. Believe me, it's not your best look. So just relax."

Alex took a big breath and let it out slowly.

"You can do it, Alex," Raymond said. "Go for it."

Alex blinked as Raymond stepped back. The sand-filled broad jump pit stretched before her like the endless Sahara Desert. The fifty-yard sprint track seemed to be a mile long, and the low hurdles might as well have been ten-foot brick walls looming in the distance.

"Concentrate, Alex!" Raymond gave her a big smile.

Alex looked at Raymond, then back at the course. Taking another deep breath, she focused on the far side of the broad jump pit and crouched, ready and waiting for Raymond's cue. She wanted to prove to everybody, especially Kelly and Ellen, that she could do it.

"On your mark," Raymond said. "Get set. Go!"

CHAPTER 4

As Alex sprang forward to make her running leap for the broad jump, she tried giving herself a small telekinetic boost. She could move objects by focusing on them intensely, but she didn't know if she could actually affect her performance in the same way. If her powers *could* help her, she didn't want to set any records that might look suspicious. She just wanted to show Kelly and her friends that they couldn't intimidate everyone.

A hush fell over the crowd as she landed. Wobbling slightly, she kept herself from stepping back with another, tiny telekinetic jolt from her mind. The jump had *felt* powerful. Had her powers helped?

"Radical!" Raymond grinned as he measured the distance. "That's the best so far!"

"Very nice, Alex." Ms. Clark beamed. "Ready for the sprint?"

Nodding, Alex jogged to the line and lowered herself into the starting position. A decisive determination had seized her, giving her what felt like superhuman power. Nothing could stop her now.

The starting gun barked, and Alex dashed forward. Spurred by an adrenaline rush, she ran on legs that seemed turbocharged. Raymond whooped as she finished the sprint. Next she headed toward the hurdle course. She felt as if there was nothing she couldn't do and she began the course. When she reached the first hurdle she sailed into the air as if she'd been doing it all her life.

Up and over. Clear!

Her friends were cheering for her, but they just went by in a blur as Alex prepared to leap over the second hurdle. She made it with inches to spare, but as she raced for the third, she began to feel the strain. She hadn't kept up an exercise routine during the weeks since school had let out, and she was running out of energy.

Keeping her eye on the hurdle, Alex focused

her thoughts on sending power into her legs. Tiring muscles surged with strength as she *thought* into them. She soared over hurdles number three and four.

"Way to go!" Raymond yelled.

Lungs bursting and heart thumping, she skimmed over number five, then headed for the last hurdle and the finish line.

"Go! Go! Go!" The crowd was on their feet, cheering her on. The sound filled Alex with an overwhelming joy and anticipation. The thrill of victory was only one hurdle and a few yards away.

With a single, ultra-concentrated effort, Alex forced her remaining mental and physical energies into leg muscles that were screaming for relief.

Up. Over. Clear!

One foot in front of the other again and again.

Alex crossed the finish line and collapsed in a heap in the middle of the track.

Lying on her back and breathless, Alex looked up into Raymond's shining face. He held out his stopwatch, but her vision was too blurred to read the dial.

"That was spectacular, Alex! A new record!"

"Really?" Alex gasped between ragged breaths. *Oops*, she thought. *Maybe I overdid it.*

"Only by three tenths of a second," Raymond said, "but it's still the best girl's time in the history of Danielle Atron Junior High. Awesome!"

"Are you all right, Alex?" Ms. Clark frowned down at her.

"Fine. Just—have to—catch my breath." Alex took the hand Ms. Clark offered.

"Good." The teacher helped Alex to her feet. "I wouldn't want anything to happen to the team star!"

"I made the team?" Alex clamped her hand over her mouth to keep from laughing out loud.

"Not officially yet." Ms. Clark smiled and winked at Alex. She seemed to be saying, "Don't worry, you made it." Alex was elated.

"Take five, Ray," Ms. Clark said. "And then we'll finish up with the last three girls."

As Ms. Clark left to confer with Mr. Hokaido, Raymond nudged Alex. "See? I was right."

"About what?"

"About using your powers," Raymond whispered, keeping his voice low so no one would overhear.

"How do you know I used my powers?" Alex

36

asked defensively. Why did Ray always assume she was using her powers?

"It's not a big deal," Raymond said. "You've got the powers; you might as well put them to good use." Raymond grinned and draped his arm over her shoulders as he steered her back toward the bleachers.

Suddenly, Alex didn't feel quite so elated about her performance. Without knowing for sure, Raymond had assumed she'd used her powers to run the course. He didn't think she could set a record on her own.

Alex's shoulders slumped as the realization hit her. Raymond was probably right. She was good, but she hadn't been training enough to be a record-breaking junior high track star.

But Alex didn't have time to worry about it. As she neared the stands, Nicole, Robyn, and Jackie rushed out to greet her.

"Way to go, Alex!" Nicole raised her hand for a high five.

"Looks like I'll be managing a winning team." Robyn was carrying a clipboard and wearing a badge that identified her as a Student Manager.

"You got the job!" Alex was happy for her friend.

"And I'm going to be Robyn's assistant,"

Jackie said eagerly. "So we'll all be working together."

"That's assuming I don't take a header off the balance beam or lose my grip on the high-low bars," Nicole said.

"You won't." Alex was absolutely certain. Nicole had natural talent. *Probably a lot more than I do,* Alex reflected.

When the track trials were completed, everyone went into the gymnasium except Jackie. The new girl excused herself, and Alex assumed she had to go to the rest room or get a drink of water.

Alex chose a seat halfway up the tier to get a good view of the gymnastics tryouts. Sitting down, she stretched her legs in front of herself to save space for Jackie.

Startling her, Scott called up from the floor, "You were great, Alex!"

"Thanks!"

Scott saw me try out! Alex realized. *And he was impressed!* Somehow that little twinge of guilt she'd been feeling was easier to push away after a compliment from Scott.

Everything was working out better than Alex had dared hope. The other three eighth-grade girls had all knocked down a hurdle, so the girl's track slot was almost certainly hers. When the kids had cheered her on, the sense of power she felt was a hundred times better than all the GC-161 side effects combined.

Winning was the only way to go.

Jackie joined her as Nicole finished her tryout routine. "How'd she do?"

"Not one mistake that I could see." Alex grinned, then realized that Jackie was flushed and out of breath. "Are you feeling okay? You look like you've got a fever."

"I'm not sick." Jackie giggled. "My ankle stopped hurting, so I ran the course again."

"And?" Alex asked anxiously, wondering if the girl had beaten her jump distance and time.

"I did much better. Not as well as you, though."

"You must be disappointed," Alex said, trying to ignore another pang of guilt. She hadn't thought about how giving herself a little telekinetic help would affect anyone else. Using her powers gave her an unfair advantage that the other kids couldn't really compete with.

"I'm not all that bummed," Jackie said. "The stress of trying to compete with my father's awesome record would have ruined the fun. And he would have pressured me to win. Now I don't have to worry about it." Jackie smiled as Nicole climbed up and sank down next to her. "I missed you, but Alex said you were perfect," Jackie said.

Too winded to talk, Nicole held up crossed fingers.

Alex relaxed. She still felt a little guilty about using her powers, but since Jackie wasn't upset about not doing well, there was no point in stressing out about it. Besides, Jackie hadn't performed well in the official tryout because of her ankle. None of the other girls had done well, either, so it wasn't as if her powers had given Alex an edge in a close contest. *Well, not exactly,* Alex told herself. She tried to stop thinking about it.

There weren't as many kids going out for the Olympic gymnastics and before long Mr. Hokaido and Ms. Clark were on the floor asking for everyone's attention. Robyn scribbled something on her clipboard, then handed it to Ms. Clark. Raymond, Scott, and the seventh-grade student coach stood behind them.

Alex tensed as the names of the seventh-grade team and alternates were called. Then Raymond stepped forward and said, "The contestants for the eighth-grade team are—"

"Here goes nothing," Nicole said.

No, Alex thought. *Here goes everything.*

"Nicole Wilson for gymnastics!" Grinning broadly, Raymond raised a victorious fist.

Nicole shrieked, then instantly composed herself.

"And Alex Mack for track."

Alex jumped up and grabbed Nicole. "We made it! We made it!"

"And Jackie Addison is the track alternate." Tucking the clipboard under his arm, Raymond whistled and applauded.

Dazed, Jackie just sat for a moment. Then she whooped and sprang to her feet. "I can't believe it! I didn't think I had a chance. Wait till I tell my dad!"

"But I thought you didn't care," Alex said to Jackie.

Jackie's answer was cut off as Raymond called the name of the alternate girl gymnast. Then the ninth-grade student coach stepped forward and announced that Scott was chosen for track. Kelly was chosen as the gymnastic contestant. Ellen acted surprised when her name was called as the winner for girl's track, but her performance had been excellent.

Mr. Hokaido blew his whistle and announced,

"Practice starts tomorrow morning. Nine o'clock sharp! Don't be late!" Then he dismissed them with a smile and a cheer for the school.

Robyn was handing out fliers by the gym exit. "Here's a list of everything you'll need for the big day."

Alex scanned the paper as they filed out of the gym. Even though she had everything she needed—the right shoes and clothes—she agreed to meet Nicole, Jackie, and Robyn at the mall later, after they had all taken showers and changed. Nicole wanted to buy a leotard and Jackie needed new running shoes. Taking leave of the three girls, she saw Raymond walking across the campus and ran to catch up to him.

"Hey, Ray! Wait up!"

"Hi, Alex. Congratulations." Raymond thumped her on the back enthusiastically. "Danielle Atron Junior High is gonna win the school trophy for sure."

"Well, I hope so."

"I *know* so." Raymond nodded emphatically, then frowned. "It's too bad about Jackie, though."

"Jackie?"

"Yeah. I let her try again, unofficially. Her second jump was only two inches short of yours and her time on the dash was just two tenths of a second slower than yours."

"That must mean she's got real potential at track and field," Alex said. Alex was impressed, and she felt another twinge of guilt about beating Jackie out for the team slot. She quickly suppressed it. Although Jackie had almost topped Alex's performance without using any powers, the new girl had made it quite clear she didn't want the stress of being on the team. *That's why she's so thrilled about being an alternate*, Alex realized suddenly. *There won't be nearly as much pressure.*

"You're like a secret weapon, Alex. The power kid." Raymond winked. "No one can beat you."

Alex could not shake an uncomfortable feeling of dismay. Raymond was right about that, too.

No one could beat her—if she used her powers.

CHAPTER 5

At dinner, Alex basked in the warmth of her parents' praise when they heard she had made the Olympic track team. She did her best to avoid Annie's questioning glare.

"I think it's wonderful that you and your friends are all participating in such a worthwhile project," Mr. Mack said to Alex. "Did you know that donating the profits to the Special Olympics was your mother's idea?" Mr. Mack scooped more mashed potatoes onto his plate and reached for the gravy that wasn't there. He grimaced as Mrs. Mack handed him a tub of low-fat margarine.

"I know," Alex said. Barbara Mack was the executive in charge of public relations for Paradise Valley Chemical, and it was not an easy job. Danielle Atron was demanding and hard to please. "It's the best PR campaign you've thought of yet, Mom."

"That's because you're so talented at what you do, Mom," Annie said. "And besides using your natural inborn ability, you work *hard* at what you do." Annie glared at Alex and mumbled, "Which is more than I can say for some people."

Alex ignored her, convinced that Annie was just jealous because she was getting all the attention for a change. Their parents didn't seem to notice the tension between them.

"What a nice compliment, Annie," Mrs. Mack said sincerely.

"Danielle's really pushing everyone at the plant to support the event," Mr. Mack said as he dipped into the tub of pale yellow spread. "I bet you'll have a sellout crowd at school."

"I hope so." Alex smiled, imagining the thunderous applause and cheers from a stadium full of people. "We really want the plant's contribution to the Special Olympic fund to be huge."

"Right," Annie muttered. "And you don't care if you win a medal or not."

"What's wrong with winning medals?" Alex

asked, annoyed. Annie had a whole shelf full of trophies from her successful science projects.

"Nothing," Annie said. "Just remember that medals aren't as important as fair play and honest effort."

"Alex knows that, Annie," Mr. Mack said.

Alex shifted uncomfortably as she met Annie's probing stare. Her sister suspected she had used her powers today when she qualified, but Alex couldn't say anything to defend herself in front of their parents.

"Awarding individual medals was Danielle's idea," Mrs. Mack said. "I just never thought Alex might actually win one. But it doesn't surprise me, Alex. We're very proud of you."

"We'll have it framed and hang it in the living room," Mr. Mack added.

"I haven't won one, yet, Dad."

"You can do anything you set your mind to, Alex," he said. "All it takes to be a winner is determination and hard work."

"Just do your best, and we'll be proud of you no matter what," Mrs. Mack said seriously.

"Absolutely." Mr. Mack glanced at his wife. "We could pack a picnic lunch on the day of the competition. Make the event a family outing."

"That's a good idea, George," Mrs. Mack said.

"I have to be there anyway to supervise the media coverage for Danielle."

Alex had had second helpings of everything for dinner to refuel after her incredible feat that afternoon. She was just pushing away from the table, stuffed to the limit, when she caught another one of her sister's glares.

"Could I see you upstairs a minute, Alex?" Annie asked.

"I have to do the dishes." Alex was not in the mood for a lecture from Annie. She was sure a week's worth of dishes would be way more fun.

"I'll do them tonight, Alex." Mrs. Mack began stacking the dirty plates. "It's a special occasion."

With no way out, Alex decided to get the unavoidable confrontation over with and started up the stairs. Annie was always reminding her about the dangers of using her powers in public. When Annie closed the bedroom door, Alex launched a counterattack before her sister said a word.

Spinning around to face her sister, she said, "I won't get caught, Annie, so stop worrying about it."

"So you did use your powers to make the

team." Annie folded her arms in front of her chest.

Alex shrugged. "I didn't mean to. A little tele-kinetic boost, that's all."

"Getting caught would serve you right!" Shaking her head, Annie perched on the edge of her bed. "How could you do something like that?"

"Like what?" Alex said. She'd decided to play innocent.

"It's cheating, Alex. Who *didn't* make the team because you telekinetically improved your performance?"

"No one! Every single girl except Jackie messed up big time. And Jackie's happy about being the alternate because she won't be under as much pressure."

"How do you know?"

"She told me."

"Maybe that's true." Annie paused, sighed, then spoke slowly to make her point. "Or maybe she didn't admit she was really disappointed because she didn't want to ruin *your* moment of triumph."

"Which is more than I can say for you!" Alex glowered at Annie. "Why can't you just let me have a little fun for a change?"

"Using your powers for personal gain is not

only dangerous, Alex, it's wrong. They give you an unfair advantage."

"That doesn't stop you." Throwing up her hands, Alex stomped toward Annie. "You're a genius, but no one gives you a hard time because you use your super brains to win scientific prizes. Everybody I know who's really good at something uses it to their own advantage."

"It's not the same thing. I compete with other brainy kids who have just as much chance of winning those scientific prizes as I do. But no one can compete with your powers because no one else has them. And that's not fair."

"Life isn't fair!" Eyes flashing, Alex vented some of the frustration she usually suppressed. "Getting doused with GC-161 wasn't fair. But I *was* doused. I *have* the powers, and not using them isn't fair, either."

"Fine!" Rising, Annie went to the door and paused before leaving. "What you do is your business, Alex, but take my word for it. Using your powers isn't right, and you will pay for it. Maybe for the rest of your life."

As the door closed behind Annie, Alex flopped on her bed and kicked off her shoes. Annie couldn't scare her. And she couldn't tell her what to do, either. The only pay Alex was going to get for using her powers was a gold medal.

Alex was the first to arrive at the stadium the next morning. By the time her friends showed up, she had jogged around the entire campus and put in fifteen minutes of warm-up exercises. Lying on the grass recovering, she grinned as Raymond peered down at her with a worried frown.

"Tired already, Alex? Practice hasn't even started."

"I'm not tired, Ray."

"You sure look pooped to me," Nicole said.

"I've just been getting warmed up." Laughing, Alex sprang to her feet and was instantly stricken with a severe cramp in her calf. Wincing, she furiously began rubbing the tightening muscle.

"What's wrong?" Robyn asked.

"Bad cramp. Guess I overdid it a little."

"Sit down," Jackie ordered. She pulled a green bottle out of her kit. "I've got just the thing to fix you up."

Alex sat, wrinkling her nose as Jackie opened the bottle and poured the foul-smelling liquid on her leg. "What is that?" Alex asked, waving a hand in front of her face.

"Liniment. My dad uses it." A penetrating warmth eased the painful tightness as Jackie massaged the liquid into Alex's muscle.

"It worked!" Relieved, Alex stood up. "Thanks, Jackie."

"Just call me Doc Addison."

"Come on, you guys," Raymond urged. "We're gonna be late."

After giving Robyn and the student coaches clipboards and instructions, Ms. Clark and Mr. Hokaido divided the twenty-four athletes into track and gymnastics squads. There were twelve kids in each squad, six primary team members and six alternates.

"Catch ya later." Nicole waved and ran to join the gymnasts, who sat in a group on the lawn.

"Uh-oh," Jackie said as she and Alex sat down with the track team. "Here comes trouble."

Alex followed Jackie's gaze and saw who she was looking at—Ellen. She passed by without a word or a glance.

"Must be our lucky day," Alex whispered.

Jackie stiffled a giggle as Mr. Hokaido blew his whistle.

"Before we start practice, I'd like to introduce

the sponsor of the county junior high Olympics." Mr. Hokaido swept his arm toward the corridor between the bleachers that led into the gym. "Ms. Danielle Atron!"

Alex's breath caught in her throat as Danielle Atron, the CEO of Paradise Valley Chemical, and Vince, the head of security, walked onto the field. The team's cheering applause was just white noise in her ears. All she could hear was Annie's ominous warning about what would happen if she used her powers to compete. It kept repeating, over and over in her head: *You will pay for it. Maybe for the rest of your life. . . .*

CHAPTER 6

Alex tensed as Danielle Atron and Vince paused before the assembled team. Vince was holding a polished glass case with a chrome frame. She wondered if a new and better GC-161 detector was hidden inside. Then she saw Dave stroll out of the corridor and climb to the top of the bleachers. He was wearing a black cap and a black jacket over his blue truck driver uniform.

Dressed in a tailored suit, Danielle gazed at the team with a tolerant smile, waiting for the polite applause to die down.

"So that's my dad's new boss," Jackie said.

Alex nodded woodenly. Why had Danielle Atron and the chief of plant security taken time away from the company to visit the Olympic team practice? And why did they come with Dave, the sole witness to the GC-161 accident that had doused Alex and changed her life forever? Only one answer came to mind. They were looking for the GC-161 kid.

And she had walked right into the trap. Alex shifted so that she sat behind a group of kids, where Danielle and her guys couldn't see her.

"Ms. Atron's really gorgeous. Even her hair is perfect." Jackie self-consciously ran a hand over her unruly dark curls. "She looks as if she just stepped off the cover of a fashion magazine."

Just stepped out of her lair is more like it, Alex thought dismally. *The lioness stalking her prey—me!* She couldn't believe the county Olympics was just another plot to catch her. She didn't want to believe it.

"Good morning, team," Ms. Atron began. "I won't keep you long. I just want to say how delighted I am that you're all participating in the county junior high Olympics. As you know, the proceeds will be donated to the Special Olympics, a worthy cause that deserves your enthusiastic support."

Cheers and whistles of support rang out from the kids on the field.

The CEO scanned their expectant faces. "I'm

confident that you'll all tackle the competition with total dedication to make this event an exciting success. Needless to say, I'd be proud and pleased if you won the school trophy, too. You are representing the school that bears my name, don't forget. I know you can do it, team. All it takes is determination and hard work." The CEO raised a fisted hand with a flourish. "Victory for Danielle Atron Junior High."

"Right on!" someone yelled.

"Victory!" another voice shouted.

The team began to cheer and stamp their feet, drawing a satisfied smile from the CEO.

Alex sighed, her brow furrowed in thought. Danielle Atron's gung-ho attitude was oddly reassuring. Maybe this event wasn't a trap after all. Maybe Ms. Atron's motive really was to raise money for the Special Olympics and get positive publicity for Paradise Valley Chemical.

The team settled down as the CEO took the glass case from Vince. She opened it and held it up. Gold, silver, and bronze medals on red, white, and blue ribbons sparkled against black velvet.

"And those of you who finish first, second, or third in your events will have these to take home." Ms. Atron motioned for silence as the team cheered again. "I know you won't disappoint me.

My associate," Ms. Atron said, nodding toward Vince, "will be stopping by periodically to see how you're doing."

"He doesn't look very enthusiastic," Jackie said.

"No, he doesn't, does he?" Alex studied Vince, Danielle's security goon, curiously. He looked totally bored as he escorted Danielle Atron to the raised stand and set the open medal case on the table.

Then Mr. Hokaido hustled everyone into their individual groups. "Okay, team! Let's show Ms. Atron what we've got!"

Uh-oh. Now I'm in trouble, Alex thought. It didn't matter whether the CEO was looking for the GC-161 kid or sponsoring the event for other reasons. The problem was that Alex couldn't use her powers while Ms. Atron and Vince were watching. And what would all the kids think after her unbelievable performance yesterday? She hoped Danielle, Vince, and Dave would leave before it was her turn.

Hanging back, Alex tried to lose herself in the crowd, but it didn't work. Ms. Clark came looking for her. "I want you and Ellen to jump first, Alex," she said. "You two were the best yesterday."

"Ummm, well, sure thing," Alex said. Panicked, she couldn't think of an excuse to back out. Ms. Clark wanted her and Ellen to go first so they could impress Danielle Atron. Alex desperately tried to think of something as she walked as slowly as possible to the jump.

Raymond ran up as she reached the broad jump pit. Ellen was already there, shaking her arms and legs to loosen up.

"It's okay, Alex," Raymond said softly.

"No, it's not, Raymond. Vince and Danielle Atron are here."

"Yeah, but I heard Ms. Clark and Mr. Hokaido talking earlier. Vince isn't here looking for you. Danielle *really* wants the school to win the Olympic meet so she can look good." Raymond lowered his voice. "She told Ms. Clark and Mr. Hokaido that if we don't win, they'll be looking for new jobs."

"Oh, that's just great—more pressure." Alex sighed.

"This is just practice anyway, Alex. Don't use your powers and you'll be fine." Raymond smiled, then jogged over to the coach.

Alex didn't share Raymond's confidence, but she didn't have a choice. She had to run the course without any telekinetic help and hope for the best.

While Alex watched, Ellen jumped on Ms. Clark's signal and landed perfectly.

"Excellent, Ellen!" The coach grinned as Raymond measured the distance and announced, "Better than yesterday."

Ellen smiled at Alex, but her eyes glinted with challenge. "Good luck, Alex," she said, but it came out like a taunt.

Taking several deep breaths, Alex stepped up to the mark. Stalling for time, she glanced toward the bleachers. Dave was idly tossing a set of keys and not paying any attention, but Vince and Danielle Atron were watching her intently. As if that wasn't enough, Scott was there too, looking on with a bunch of older kids.

"Come on, Alex," Raymond said. "You can do it."

No I can't, Alex thought as she took off running. She knew her jump was way short of Ellen's mark before she hit the ground. Losing her balance on her landing, she fell forward onto her hands. Getting up, she felt as if a million eyes were staring at her.

"Too bad, Alex. Better luck next time." Ellen smiled reassuringly, but there was triumph in her voice.

Embarrassed, Alex hung her head as she joined Ellen at the sprint and hurdle track. Alex started counting in her head and taking slow, deep breaths to calm herself. If she started glowing now, Vince would certainly notice.

"Are you feeling ill today, Alex?" Ms. Clark asked.

Saved! Alex quickly said, "My stomach's a little upset—"

"She had a major cramp in her leg this morning, too," Raymond added for good measure.

"It's probably the pressure," Ellen said with a concerned frown. "You'll get over it before the meet, Alex. If you try really hard."

"I'll be okay, Ms. Clark," Alex said, clenching her jaw.

Next Alex stepped up to her lane for the sprint course and got in her starting position.

The gun went off. Alex ran as hard as she could, but Ellen finished the sprint several yards ahead of her.

The hurdle course was next. Alex was still breathing hard as she and Ellen took their marks. When the gun went off, Ellen shot out ahead of Alex, then cleared the first hurdle in perfect form.

Alex knocked it over and almost fell.

"Get with it, Mack!" someone yelled.

Unnerved, Alex grazed the top of the second hurdle and knocked down the third.

Ahead of her, Ellen cleared number four. The team cheered.

The memory of yesterday's triumph was fading fast for Alex. Desperate to hold on to that wonderful sensation she'd felt when everybody cheered for her, she concentrated with all the mental power she could muster. She could redeem herself over the last three hurdles with a telekinetic boost.

After all, no one had noticed anything unusual yesterday.

Everyone—the team, the coaches, and even Danielle Atron—was so intent on winning, they weren't looking for reasons to question her newly discovered talent for track.

The energies churned in her mind.

All she had to do was channel the power into her legs.

She didn't have to be a loser.

It was worth the risk.

Alex focused on her legs. Too late, she realized that she was too nervous and tired to control the energy flow. Instead of a small jolt, *all* the telekinetic power she generated surged into her legs as she sprang.

She cleared the fourth hurdle—by an impossible three feet!

CHAPTER 7

Everyone in the stadium gasped.

Surprise and terror struck Alex in mid air. The height of her jump startled her, breaking her concentration. She almost felt as if she were flying! Arms and legs flailing, she belly flopped into the dirt. But that humiliation was nothing compared to the horrifying certainty that her life was about to take a downhill plunge from which there was no return.

Ever.

Vince and Danielle Atron must have seen the monstrous leap. They would test her to find out how she had done it. They would find GC-161 in her system and she would become an experimental prisoner in the plant for the rest of her life.

Squeals and laughter rose around her. But embarrassment was the least of her worries. Sputtering and coughing dirt out of her mouth, Alex raised her head as Raymond fell on his knees beside her.

"Are you crazy?" Frantic, Raymond looked over his shoulder.

"It's all over, Ray." A tear rolled down Alex's cheek, streaking the dust that covered her face. "Danielle's gonna haul me into her lab and—"

"Shh. Maybe not." Taking her arm, Raymond helped her up as Ms. Clark hurried over.

"What happened, Alex?" The coach frowned anxiously.

"I'm sorry, Ms. Clark. I just—"

"Got another cramp." Raymond shot a warning look at Alex. "She caught her foot on the hurdle and dove into the ground."

"Did you break anything?" Ms. Clark asked.

Confused, Alex shook her head, then glanced past the coach when the crowd gasped again.

"He's gonna fall!" A girl shrieked.

Dave, Danielle Atron's driver, was dangling off the end of the high bleachers. He was hanging on to the railing with one arm and trying to climb back up. Scott and another boy raced up to him, took hold of his arms, and pulled him to safety.

"Can't you do anything right, Dave?" Vince shouted.

Collapsing on a seat, Dave held up the keys and grinned, "I didn't lose the keys, Vince."

Tapping her foot in disgust, Danielle Atron glared at Dave, then turned on Vince. "I never should have let this idiot fill in as my chauffeur today."

"He was the only available driver with the proper license, Ms. Atron," Vince explained.

"The next time my regular driver calls in sick get someone else," Ms. Atron snapped. "Anyone else!"

Hope flickered through Alex's frightened daze. Vince hadn't brought Dave to the practice to identify the GC-161 kid. The truck driver was substituting for Danielle Atron's sick chauffeur.

Alex started as Ms. Clark put a gentle hand on her arm. "I'm sorry I didn't see you jump, Alex. I could have pointed out where you went wrong if I had seen it. But when that clown dropped his keys and fell trying to grab them, I was watching him instead of you."

"Really?" Inhaling sharply, Alex stared at Raymond.

"Everybody was watching him," Raymond said emphatically.

"Everybody?"

"Everybody." Raymond smiled. "Except me."

Alex grinned broadly. *Vince and Danielle didn't see my impossible jump! I'm in luck! And most of the kids didn't see it either.*

Ms. Riley insisted that Alex sit out the rest of the practice. As she headed for the bleachers, Danielle Atron went into the school with Mr. Hokaido. Alex paused by a small stand where the case of medals had been placed. Sunlight reflected off the shiny surfaces of the medals, and the red, white, and blue ribbons looked crisp and clean. The gold first place award gleamed brilliantly.

Suddenly a hand reached over and slammed the case closed.

Alex jumped back. Her heart began to race and she looked up into Vince's steely blue eyes. *Maybe he saw me after all!*

"You're Gary Mick's daughter, aren't you?" Vince asked.

Alex just nodded. Vince never remembered her father's name, and correcting him seemed like a really bad idea at the moment.

"Well, you can stop drooling over these medals, kid. You don't stand a chance. What you just did out there was the worst athletic demonstration I have ever seen."

"I—uh, my legs cramped," Alex stammered.

"Get over it. There are no acceptable excuses for failure." Vince's eyes narrowed. "If the school trophy is lost, Ms. Atron will be very unhappy. When Ms. Atron's unhappy, I'm unhappy. And when I'm unhappy, people pay."

"Yes, sir."

Tucking the medal case under his arm, Vince strode down the corridor toward the gym.

Alex's first reaction was relief. Raymond was right. Atron and her employees were here today to make sure that the students won the event. Not to find out the truth about Alex and haul her away. But Alex also felt as though the medal had been snatched from her grasp forever, and she wanted it more than anything. Annie's side of the bedroom was full of awards she had won for scientific and academic achievement and excellence. All Alex had was a dinky honorable mention trophy for the sack race at Camp Wahooie. The big trophy she had won last year was for milking a stupid cow. Then there was the plaque she'd won for the Paradise Valley cleanup project.

This was different. This was competitive sports. The best athletes from every school in the county would be competing in the junior high Olympics for those medals.

The only way to get a gold medal was to win one.

And the only way Alex knew she could win one was to use her powers.

Was winning worth the risk of getting caught by Danielle Atron? And if she won by using her powers, could she live with the awful truth that she had won dishonestly?

Alex thought about her messy situation for most of the evening. Her parents were out, and Annie was working on the voltage helmet. Although Alex needed someone to talk to, she didn't need a lecture, so she had avoided Annie and her electrodes since getting home.

Her friends couldn't help, either, and not only because they didn't know about GC-161 and her powers. Nicole and Jackie were so tired, they said they were going to bed early, and Robyn had schedules to write.

Alex ate popcorn and watched TV, hoping it would distract her. It didn't. When Raymond dropped by to see how she was doing, Alex was overjoyed. He was probably the only person in the whole world who could help her find a solution to a problem that didn't seem to have one.

"There's got to be a way out of this," Raymond said. He sprawled on the couch with the bowl of popcorn.

"What?" Frustrated, Alex stretched out on the floor with her hands under her head. "I'm not good enough to win without using my powers, but I can't use them when Vince and Danielle are around. They make me too nervous to concentrate, and I have to concentrate harder than usual to control my boosted jumps."

Raymond sat up suddenly. "Vince and Danielle Atron will be at the Olympic meet."

"I know."

"So what are you going to do? You made the team and everyone's counting on you." Raymond hesitated as the seriousness of the situation finally made an impact. "If we don't win, Ms. Clark and Mr. Hokaido could lose their jobs!"

"Don't you think I've thought of that?" More angry at herself than at Raymond, Alex rolled over onto her stomach. "There's only one thing I can do."

"Right. Get over being nervous in front of

Vince so you can use your powers." Raymond tilted his head back and dropped popcorn into his open mouth.

"No. I can't risk messing up again the way I did today." Alex shuddered, remembering just how close she had come to ruining her life that afternoon.

"I don't understand," Raymond said. "You can't clear all those hurdles without the powers. How else are you going to do it?"

"With hard work and determination, Ray." Jumping up, Alex began to pace. "I'm not in very good shape right now, but I've got almost two weeks. If I train really hard every day, I think I can improve enough to make a difference. Maybe even win!"

"I don't know."

"I can do it, Ray." The more Alex thought about it, the more certain she became. "I hate to admit it, but Annie was right about my powers giving me an unfair advantage. Winning a gold medal won't *mean* anything if I use them."

"That's progress," Annie said from the hall. "When you've got a minute, Alex, I need you in the garage."

Alex blinked with surprise as Annie left without another word. It wasn't like her to walk away when Alex saw things her way. Usually she got at least a snide comment or a lecture.

"We're doomed." Raymond slumped and sighed.

"Not necessarily." Alex sank onto the couch beside him. "Even if I come in third, the school will still get points."

"I guess, but if you only place third and the Greenfield runner wins, we could still lose. Ms. Clark has the performance stats from all the school track meets last year. The Greenfield girls are fast. Except for you, Jackie is the only one who came close to matching the eighth-grade Greenfield girls' times and jump distances today. Jackie could *win.*"

"What are you saying, Ray?"

"She didn't knock down a single hurdle, either," Raymond muttered thoughtfully. He stood up suddenly and peered down at Alex with a troubled expression. "If you hadn't used your powers to make the team, Jackie would be *on* the team and not just the alternate."

Alex faltered. "But she said she didn't care."

"Come on, Alex. Do you really think Jackie would have refused a team slot if she'd gotten it?" Raymond shook his head and avoided looking at her.

"Are you mad at me?" Alex asked, genuinely perplexed. Raymond was always trying to get her to use her powers. He usually thought it was totally radical, and a lot less work than doing things the hard way.

"Not mad exactly. It's just that I never really thought about whether using your powers was fair. I mean, Jackie should be on the team, not you."

"But Jackie didn't want the pressure of competing with her dad's amazing record," Alex argued stubbornly. "That's what she told me, Ray. I swear."

"Maybe." Sighing, Raymond turned toward the door. "I gotta go. See you in the morning."

After Raymond left, Alex tried to watch TV again, but she couldn't stop thinking about his change in attitude. He hadn't complained about the fairness of using her powers before she had decided to compete without them. It was only when he saw how bad she was at track that his conscience started bothering him.

Still, he had a valid point. If she hadn't given herself a telekinetic boost, Jackie would be on the primary team.

Disturbed, Alex wandered aimlessly through the house for a few minutes, then went to the garage. Annie was sure to press the issue, and Alex needed a good argument to vent her frustrations and sort out her thoughts.

"This won't take long," Annie said, pointing Alex toward the stool. "I just have to make a few preliminary calibrations."

Minutes passed in total silence as Annie placed the voltage regulator helmet on Alex's head and fitted the electrodes.

Finally, Alex couldn't stand it any longer. "Don't you have something to say?"

"Like what?"

"Like what a rotten person I am for using my powers to make the Olympic team."

Annie looked Alex in the eye. "Alex, you're almost fifteen years old. If you don't know the difference between right and wrong by now, there's nothing I can say to change it."

Thanks a lot, Alex thought miserably. When Annie argued, it was easy to ignore the fact that she might be right. But like Raymond, Annie was appealing to Alex's own sense of integrity and fair play, and she couldn't ignore that.

How much was a gold medal worth?

CHAPTER 8

Alex tossed and turned all that night, haunted by dreams of winning gold medals that turned to dust in her hands. When she arrived at practice the next morning, she had every intention of quitting the team. Winning a gold medal was not worth losing her self-respect. Fair was fair, and Jackie deserved the team slot. Alex didn't deserve it because she had not won it honestly.

But nothing went as Alex had planned.

She told Robyn she was dropping out of the competition because she had promised to work with Annie on a very important, top-secret project. She said she didn't have time to devote her full attention to the project and the team, too.

Robyn was certain she was afraid of failing

and letting the team down because of her leg cramps the previous day. The cramps were probably just a physical manifestation of her fears anyway, Robyn decided, and the best way to conquer fear was to face it head on. Alex had been counting on Robyn to be her good old gloomy self and let her drop out. No such luck. For some reason Robyn had the optimism and determination of a cheerleader today.

Ms. Clark insisted that the team needed Alex to win the school trophy. Everyone got nervous and questioned their abilities before a major competition, she said. The coach couldn't tell Alex that her job was at stake, and Alex couldn't explain that she had used telekinesis to perform so well at the tryouts. So Alex's conversation with Ms. Clark went nowhere fast.

Nicole wouldn't let her off the hook, either. Rich and famous movie stars and professional athletes donated their time and talent to the Special Olympics. Alex had a moral obligation to help kids less fortunate than herself, too.

Jackie looked stricken when Alex suggested that maybe they should switch places. Her father was delighted that she was the alternate. If she was on the team, she wouldn't have any fun because she'd spend the next two weeks worrying herself sick.

Raymond overheard that conversation and agreed that Alex didn't have any choice but to throw herself into practice and compete just like the other kids. Maybe she would improve. Then, as the eighth-grade student coach, he set about making sure that she did.

Determined to succeed, Alex didn't complain when Raymond made her do extra sit-ups and additional laps around the track during practice. Every day he asked for a little more effort, and she gave it to him. Rising at five o'clock each morning, she got to the stadium before the rest of the team to leap hurdles. After practice she jogged for hours in the backyard and around the block to build up her muscles and wind. Exhausted, she was in bed every night by nine and slept soundly until the alarm went off and the brutal routine started over again. She even learned to ignore Vince when he showed up to talk to the coaches about the team's progress. Anyway, she didn't have much to worry about, since she wasn't using her supernatural powers—just her natural powers, which were growing stronger every day.

Inspired by Alex's dedicated determination,

Mr. Mack decided he needed to get back in shape. After two grueling evenings of jogging around the neighborhood and not being able to keep up, he began pacing her in the car, providing water and moral support as he rode down the street beside her while she jogged. Her mother did some research in the library and began preparing meals like those served to real Olympic athletes. Their enthusiasm and encouragement spurred Alex to work even harder.

Except for the few hours Annie needed her in the garage, Alex didn't do anything for two weeks but eat, sleep, and train, train, train. As the county Olympics drew near, she was sure of only one thing. Win or lose, she had given the effort everything she had.

The day before the Olympic event, Alex arrived at the stadium early, as usual. She felt great as she jogged across the campus. Spring-coiled muscles carried her effortlessly over the ground, and she wasn't even breathing hard when she reached the gate. Filled with energy and confidence, Alex headed for the track.

Jackie was there ahead of her, sitting cross-legged on the ground, staring at the track.

"Hey, Jackie!" Alex waved as she dashed over. "What's up?"

"Nothing. Just thinking." Sighing, Jackie propped her chin in her hands.

"About what?" Alex asked, sitting down beside her.

"It's my dad. Last night he decided to polish all his track medals. It was a not-very-subtle hint."

Alex's heart fluttered. "He's disappointed, huh?"

"I suppose." Jackie shrugged. "He wants to see me be a winner, just like him. He says I'll never know how good I can be unless I try. To be honest, I can't help wondering, either. I mean about how I'd do if I actually did compete tomorrow."

Taking a deep breath, Alex nodded. Jackie had worked just as hard as the kids who knew they would compete. And so had all the other alternates. "Anything can happen tomorrow, Jackie. You might get to compete, you never know."

"The only way I'd get to run is if something happened to you, Alex. What kind of person would I be if I wished that on someone else? Especially someone who's been so nice to me."

Alex froze, stricken by the girl's words. Jackie really did want to compete, but not if it meant hurting someone else's chances at winning. She really was being considerate of Alex.

Alex shriveled inside. During the tryouts, she hadn't stopped to think about how using her powers to make the team would hurt someone else. Then she had justified her actions because Jackie seemed genuinely glad that she hadn't been picked.

Jackie smiled and said, "Oh, well. If I were on the team, I'd probably lose, and then my dad would be totally disappointed."

Alex couldn't tell how Jackie really felt, since it didn't seem that she'd made her mind up yet whether or not she wanted to compete. But Alex suspected that Annie was right. Jackie was just saying she didn't want to compete so nobody would feel sorry for her for being just an alternate. She didn't want to spoil everyone else's fun. Alex couldn't force the girl to take the eighth-grade track slot, but the whole situation was troubling.

"What's this?" Raymond demanded.

Alex looked up to find Raymond looking down at her with a grim and disapproving expression. "What's what?"

"This sitting around stuff. The meet is tomorrow, guys. No time to waste. Let's go, go, go!"

"Yes, sir!" Giggling, Jackie saluted and sprang to her feet.

Alex jumped up and stood nose to nose with Raymond. "Slave driver."

"It worked, didn't it?" Raymond grinned and twirled his whistle. "You've never been this fit in your life."

"True." Alex smiled.

"Ten laps. Starting now." Folding his arms, Raymond silently dared her to argue.

"Easy." Shaking a slight kink out of her leg, Alex jogged onto the track. Jackie matched her stride for stride, and Alex resolved that somehow the new girl would race tomorrow. Alex had made the team unfairly and for selfish reasons. She owed Jackie a chance at her own moment of Olympic glory.

"Alex."

"Huh?" Waking up suddenly, Alex sat bolt upright. The TV remote slid off her chest onto the floor.

"I didn't mean to scare you, honey," Mrs. Mack said. "If you're so tired, why don't you just go to bed?"

"Can't." Alex picked up the remote, then

stretched out on the couch again. "I'm too nervous about tomorrow."

"Of course you are, but you can't run your best if you don't get a good night's sleep."

"I'll be fine. Promise."

"Okay." Mrs. Mack sighed. "Maybe we should just stay home tonight. The Hartfords will understand. I should make you a decent dinner instead of feeding you leftovers on the eve of your Olympic debut."

"It's not a problem, Mom. They're leftovers from a very healthy Olympic training table meal, right?"

"Yes, you're right." Noticing the cordless telephone handset on the coffee table, Mrs. Mack put it back on the base. "Remember to hang up the phone, Alex. You know I hate it when the batteries go dead in the middle of an important call."

"Sorry. Have fun." Alex was glad her parents were going out. She didn't want them fussing over her and making a big deal out of how proud they were. If they did, she might be tempted to change her plans for tomorrow.

Flipping through the channels, Alex finally settled on a vintage science fiction movie that might be good for a few laughs. She needed something to take her mind off her decision to give up her place on the team. Losing her own chance to bring home a medal was a total bummer, but winning at Jackie's expense would only tarnish the prize. She'd never be able to look at it without knowing she had betrayed the Olympic spirit, her friends, and herself.

"You're awfully calm for someone who's going to race the best junior high athletes in the county tomorrow," Annie said as she entered the living room.

"That's because I won't be racing anybody tomorrow." Alex yawned. "But you can't tell anyone."

"Having second thoughts about how you made the team, huh?"

"More like fourth or fifth thoughts. Maybe even tenth." Alex looked away from the TV and saw the white football helmet tucked under Annie's arm. "What's that?"

"Dad's old football helmet."

"I know that." Alex rolled her eyes and sat up again. "What are you doing with it?"

Annie turned the helmet upside down. "I hollowed it out and installed the voltage regulator helmet inside. Except for this gauge and this switch on the back, it looks like an ordinary football helmet. It'll be easier to explain than wired electrodes in case anyone sees you wearing it."

"Uh-huh. And why would anyone see me wearing it?" Alex asked suspiciously.

"Mom and Dad might come home before I've completed the test."

"I'm not wearing that thing tonight." As Annie moved to put the helmet on her head, Alex blocked it with her arm. "I've had a hard day and tomorrow's going to be worse. I just want to relax."

"All you have to do is sit here, which you're doing anyway. I just want to monitor the normal flow of electricity through your system for a while." Annie threw the switch on the back of the helmet and held it out. "See. It's on a monitor and the rheostat is turned off."

"What's a rheostat?" Alex scowled as she checked out the intricate digital display. "It's set on high."

"It's a device that varies the resistance of an electrical circuit without interrupting the circuit. Like the dimmer switch on the hall light."

"Oh." Alex stifled another yawn with the back of her hand. "Sounds dangerous."

Annie sighed, losing patience. "Only if you're hooked up to an electrical current, which you're not. So humor me and cooperate. This device might give me information that will save your life someday."

"Can't argue with that, I guess." Alex had to fight to keep from nodding off as Annie adjusted the helmet.

"Does Jackie know that you're backing out tomorrow?" Annie asked as she attached electrodes to Alex's hands and legs.

"No, but it's just as well. This way she doesn't lose any sleep tonight because she's stressed out about the games."

"Looks like you could use some sleep yourself," Annie said as she finished and headed toward the stairs. "I've got to bring my notes up to date. I'll check on you in an hour or so."

"Sure." Alex stared at the TV for a moment, but soon her head fell forward onto her chest and she dozed off. The weight of the helmet strained her neck, and she snapped awake just long enough to throw her head back against the couch. She heard a click and her eyes slowly closed again.

The ringing phone sounded like a distant bell tolling in a dream. Alex picked up the handset in a sleepy daze, then realized she couldn't put it to her ear because of the helmet. She turned on the speakerphone switch. "Hello?" She mumbled.

"Hey, Alex. It's Robyn."

"Uh-huh."

"Ms. Atron is donating matching shorts and tops for the team, so you need to be at the school stadium a half hour earlier than planned. Gotta lot of calls to make, so I'll see you in the a.m. Seven-thirty sharp. Bye."

"Early. Right." *Not a problem*, Alex thought. She had been getting up at five for almost two weeks. *No wonder I can't keep my eyes open.*

Turning off the speakerphone, Alex reached to put the handset back on its base. She didn't notice that it missed and fell onto the table and that her hand settled into the charging cradle instead. Resting her helmeted head on the arm of the couch, she tucked her legs underneath her. A faint buzzing sounded in her ears, and she realized it was the phone. Too tired to move, her last thought before falling into a deep sleep was that her mom would be really upset because the batteries in the cordless phone weren't charged.

CHAPTER 9

Annie stopped writing and glanced at her watch.

Three hours! She had been so intent on her work, she had forgotten all about the time and her experiment with Alex. Finishing her last note, Annie hurried downstairs. Her sister was sound asleep, still wearing the helmet.

"Wake up." Annie gently shook her arm, but Alex didn't stir. "Alex?"

Annie jumped as the front door opened and her parents walked in.

No problem, Annie thought as she turned to greet them. *How hard can it be to explain why Alex is sleeping on the couch with a football helmet on her head?*

"Hi, Mom. Dad." Annie smiled. "Have a good time?"

"Too good." Mr. Mack yawned. "I had no idea it was so late."

"Look at Alex. She should be in bed," Mrs. Mack said. Shaking her head, she reached for the handset that had fallen from Alex's hand. "Why is she wearing your father's football helmet?" she asked Annie.

"Uh—she found it in the garage," Annie said, noticing that the electrode on Alex's hand was resting on the charge-nodes in the handset cradle. "Maybe she decided to wear it for luck in the track meet tomorrow or something." Annie put her hand out to take the handset from her mother. If Mrs. Mack tried to hang it up, she'd see the electrodes attached to Alex. That would be a little harder to explain.

"I think that's sweet." Mrs. Mack put the phone handset in Annie's outstretched hand.

"Well, I hope it brings her more luck than it did me." Mr. Mack sighed. "I decided I wasn't cut out for the company football team after the first corporate league game."

"You were lucky you didn't break any bones," Mrs. Mack said.

"I'll say." Mr. Mack peered down at Alex. "Looks uncomfortable, but she's out like a light."

"I'd better get her upstairs." Putting down her purse, Mrs. Mack stepped around the end of the couch.

"I'll do it, Mom," Annie said quickly. "You look beat."

"Thanks, Annie. Don't forget to set her alarm. She has to be at the school by eight."

After her parents had gone upstairs, Annie shook Alex a little harder. Alex mumbled and swatted her sister's hand away. Muttering, Annie pushed her into a sitting position and gasped. The switch on the helmet had been moved from monitor to rheostat. She had no idea what effect that might have on her sister.

"Alex?" Annie ripped the electrodes off Alex's hands and legs, then lifted off the helmet. Alex's hair crackled and fanned out from her head like a high-voltage fright wig. Annie blinked, then shrugged. Static electricity wasn't lethal.

"Speak to me, Alex. Are you all right?"

"Go 'way." Alex lay down again and curled into a ball. "Leave me 'lone."

"Well, that sounds just like our Alex. I guess she's okay." Sighing, Annie considered dragging her sister upstairs, then decided against it. Alex was sleeping soundly and didn't seem to be suffering any ill effects from the helmet. None that couldn't be controlled with a couple of tons of hair products, anyway. She'd just have to get up early and run some tests before Alex left for the stadium. Making a mental note to reset the alarm for seven-fifteen, Annie went to bed.

Alex sat up, instantly wide awake. *I'm late!* Jumping off the couch, she dashed into the kitchen. The wall clock read six-fifteen. Whew! She wasn't late, but she didn't have time to waste. After pouring herself some orange juice, she tiptoed upstairs to the bathroom.

Clean shorts and a tank top, new socks, and running shoes were stacked on the hamper.

Mom. Smiling sadly, Alex set down her glass and picked up the shoes. She hated disappointing her parents. They had been looking forward to watching her race for two weeks. Her dad had even spent one whole night trying to decide where to hang the medal she wouldn't win. They would never know the real reason why she didn't compete, but she knew they would be just as proud of her for doing the right thing.

Sighing, Alex, went into the bathroom, turned on the shower, then pulled her sweatshirt over her head. Hair and fabric crackled, and a few sparks flew. Alex stared at herself in the mirror.

Her hair was a flyaway fright. Extra conditioner was an absolute must this morning.

Pressed for time, Alex set a record for taking a shower and dressing. She was back in the kitchen at six-forty, scribbling a note to let her mother know that she was riding her bike to the stadium and would see everyone there later. As she put down the pencil, she touched the toaster.

An electrical bolt leaped from her fingers and sizzled through the appliance. The toaster jumped off the counter and, landing with a crash, started to smoke.

At the same instant, Alex felt a telekinetic itch in her head. Before she could control it, the energy fled outward and hit the blender, turning it on. Surprised, Alex unplugged the toaster and turned off the blender. What had triggered that? She hadn't deliberately released the electrical charge or the telekinetic command.

Disturbed, Alex slowly looked around the kitchen. All was quiet. Must be nerves, she decided. Even though she wasn't going to race, she was apprehensive about her acting abilities. First she had to convince everyone that she had injured herself. Then she had to avoid being checked out too thoroughly by the medics at the first-aid station. Right now, she had to worry about anxiety-related telekinetic spasms and electrical bolts.

As she turned to leave, Alex noticed that her note was sticking to her tank top. Static electricity crackled as she peeled the slip of paper off and placed it back on the counter.

It slid toward her as if it had a will of its own.

"I don't have time for this," Alex mumbled. Setting a salt shaker on the note, she grabbed her backpack from the kitchen table. As she opened the door, the edge of the curtain curled up and plastered itself to her shorts.

Exasperated, Alex dashed outside. Her mom must have forgotten to put an anti-static sheet in the dryer when she did the laundry. Hoping the effect would wear off by the time she reached the stadium, Alex hopped on her bike.

Clinging clothes are the least of my problems, Alex thought as she pedaled through the empty streets. The gymnastics events were scheduled for the morning hours and track for the afternoon. She'd have to wait until after lunch to implement her plan. It would only work if she faked her injury just before her events started. That way, she wouldn't have time to recover and Jackie wouldn't have time to stress out.

Taking a shortcut through the vacant lot, Alex

arrived at the school parking lot with fifteen minutes to spare. Although it was still early, the bike rack was almost full. Dropping her backpack, Alex chose a vacant spot in the middle of the rack and grabbed the metal bar to steady herself.

A huge zapper shot from her fingers. Bike frames rattled and pedals turned as electricity shot through the metal rack.

Panic seized Alex as a telekinetic burst picked up her bike and shoved it forward into the rack. An instant later, a hot flash radiated through her arms and legs. Then a silvery, liquid film rippled across her skin, as if she were about to morph. She stared at her watery fingers as they became solid again.

Alex shuddered. Her powers were going berserk!

The sound of giggling drew Alex's alarmed attention. Two girls were walking toward her. One of them pointed at her, then looked away when she caught Alex's eye. The other one had her hand over her mouth and was trying not to laugh.

Alex desperately tried to calm down. Having her powers suddenly run amuck was frightening, but not as terrifying as having witnesses.

Kids talked, especially if they thought something weird was going on. Eventually, stories about the girl with liquid skin would reach Danielle Atron.

Smiling tightly as the girls drew closer, Alex wondered if she had lucked out again. Maybe they hadn't noticed anything strange. They were amused, but not upset. Then they passed in front of her.

Both girls squealed and pointed at each other as their hair flared out from their heads. Their sweatsuits whooshed against their bodies as though sucked in by a giant vacuum cleaner. Clamping their hands over their flyaway hair, they dashed for the school.

Did I do that, too?

Bewildered, Alex looked down at herself. Her clothes were covered with leaves, grass, and bits of paper. No wonder they had laughed at her. She looked like a walking trash can. She must have been collecting loose debris during the entire bike ride.

Why?

Obviously, she was generating some kind of super-electrical field. And it wasn't difficult to figure out how that had happened, either. Somehow, Annie's helmet had overloaded her with electrical energy, and the supercharge was causing uncontrolled bursts of her powers. Even worse, anyone who came near her was affected by an overdose of static electricity.

Without hesitating, Alex pulled her bike out of the rack. There was no way she would stay at the stadium. After she got home, she'd have Annie call Ms. Clark to explain that she was sick. Different plan. Same results. Jackie would compete in her place and everything would be fine—as soon as Annie figured out how to get rid of the extra electricity.

Right now, it was more important to get away before anyone saw her. Not only did her clothes look as if she'd slept in the town dump, her powers were going crazy without warning.

"There's Alex!"

Heart sinking, Alex glanced back. The entire Danielle Atron Junior High team was jogging toward her across the parking lot.

Behind them, Vince and Danielle Atron stepped out of a big, black luxury car.

CHAPTER 10

Shoving her bike back into the rack and snatching up her backpack, Alex turned and ran. She didn't know how she was going to explain running away, but it was bound to be easier than explaining a bad-hair-day epidemic or why everyone who got close to her was suddenly stricken with major static cling.

Nicole and Jackie called out, but Alex did not look back or slow down. Sparks flew off the metal gate as she charged into the stadium. Attracting more bits of debris as she ran, Alex headed straight for the corridor between the bleachers that led to the gym.

"Alex! What happened to you?" Ms. Clark gasped as Alex whizzed past the judges' table.

"Fell off my bike!" Alex shouted, skidding as she cornered the bleachers into the fenced passageway. At full speed she burst through the wooden, double doors of the gym without touching the metal handle and almost collided with Mr. Hokaido.

The startled gymnastics coach stopped as Alex swerved and ducked into the locker room on the right. "That's the—"

"Wrong one!" Alex dashed back out the door and across the hall in front of him. "Sorry!"

Rushing into the girls' locker room, Alex raced past the lockers and sinks to the end stall. She braked before the metal door. Tossing her backpack in ahead of her, she crawled underneath the door instead of opening it. She couldn't risk touching the door and unleashing a super-zapper in the locker room. Almost everything was made of metal and the results might be catastrophic.

Sitting on the lid of the porcelain toilet, she used her foot to close the door and push the bolt. The rubber-soled sneakers prevented the flow of electricity, just as the rubber grips and tires on her bike and the plastic shower knobs had.

Alex paused to catch her breath and decide what to do next.

Thirty seconds later, Nicole ran in. "Are you in here, Alex?"

Breathless and panicked, Alex groaned aloud.

"Did you find her?" Jackie asked as she came through the door.

"I think she's down there," Nicole said. "I just heard someone, and she doesn't sound good."

Sick! Alex slapped her forehead. That was her original plan, which she'd forgotten all about in her panic. Being sick to her stomach was perfect. That would explain why she had left the parking lot in such a hurry and raced to the toilet. And it was the perfect excuse to explain why she'd have to go home and desert the team.

"I'm here, Nicole, but I don't feel too good." Alex moaned pitifully.

Footsteps padded across the tile. Alex stood up as two sets of sneakers paused outside the stall. She quickly turned to face the toilet, just in case one of them looked under the door to make sure she was all right.

"What's the problem, Alex?" Nicole asked.

"I think maybe I caught the flu."

"Overnight?"

"It happens," Jackie said.

Alex gagged. "I feel terrible."

"It's just nerves," Nicole said impatiently.

"You've worked like a maniac for two weeks and now the big day is here. Win or lose, this is it. Of course you feel sick."

"It happens to me all the time," Jackie said. "Only I would have been sick every day for the past two weeks if I had to compete today."

"Are you coming out?" Nicole asked. "We should be warming up."

"Just give me a few minutes, okay?" Arguing with Nicole was futile, Alex decided. She just wanted the girls to leave so she could go home before something truly disastrous happened.

"Okay. We've got to change anyway."

Change? Several more girls entered, and the locker room echoed with their excited chatter. Then Alex remembered Robyn's phone call last night and realized that everyone had to change into the team uniforms Danielle Atron had given them.

Ellen's voice rang out above the din. "Where's Alex?"

Someone else laughed. "She was running so fast, she's probably in the next county by now."

"Could be," Ellen agreed. "There's no Olympics in the next county."

"Poor thing," Kelly said with phony concern.

"Some people have a hard time handling the pressure."

Alex fumed. It had never occurred to her that anyone would think she was afraid to compete. Between her decision to let Jackie run and her renegade powers, there wasn't anything she could do to change the other girls' assumption, either. Nicole lowered her voice to talk through the stall door. "You'll be all right, Alex. See you on the field."

"Here's your uniform," Jackie said.

Alex glanced down as Jackie pushed the folded top and shorts into the stall. Blue with red trim, the satiny fabric reacted to her static-electrical field and started to puff up. Quickly, Alex grabbed the clothes from the floor.

As Nicole and Jackie left, Kelly spoke up again. "What did you do to your hair, Jackie?"

"Gosh! Look at it!" Jackie exclaimed.

Alex knew Jackie had just caught sight of herself in the mirror. Sighing, Alex sat back down and drew her legs up to wait. She passed the time picking paper and grass off her clothes.

Ten minutes later the locker room door banged closed and quiet prevailed. Another minute passed before Alex decided the coast was clear. Still sitting on the toilet, she raised her foot to open the door. As she slid the bolt back, she lost her balance. Before she realized what she was doing, her reflexes made her grab the metal paper holder.

A monster zapper flew from her fingertips to the dispenser, triggering a telekinetic surge that rocked Alex back against the wall. Then several things happened at once.

The zap of electricity hit the door with a thunderous crack and, like a lightning bolt, lit up all the stalls as it ripped down the row.

Alex shuddered as various parts of her body morphed and unmorphed in a rapid, random pattern.

A telekinetic surge struck the toilet bowl and sped through the plumbing. All the seats began to bang up and down as five toilets flushed at once.

And then Danielle Atron walked through the door of the locker room.

CHAPTER 11

"Is someone in here?" Ms. Atron called out as the locker room door clunked closed.

Stop! Alex deliberately projected a telekinetic command at the pounding toilet seats and flushing water. They stopped, leaving the room in silence. Alex let out a relieved whoosh of air, but then her left leg tingled and turned to jelly.

An agonizing few seconds passed without a sound.

Clutching the team uniform to her chest, Alex bit her lip. Her leg solidified, but a liquid wave rippled down her right arm. She tensed as high heels clicked on the tiled floor. Ms. Atron stopped outside the door.

"Who are you? What's the problem?"

"Alex Mack. I—uh—got sick to my stomach."

"That's just nerves. You'd better hurry or you'll miss the parade."

"I'm not dressed, yet," Alex stammered. Staying calm was absolutely necessary if she wanted to get out of the locker room without the CEO noticing anything unusual. The new uniform would help. It wasn't covered with lint and debris. She peeled off her top and slipped the new blue-and-red team shirt over her head.

Ms. Atron began to pace back and forth. "Stress very often manifests itself with physical symptoms. A high percentage of corporate executives suffer stress-related illnesses. I see it all the time at the plant."

That's because they work for you, Alex thought, pulling off her old shorts. She had to stand up to pull on the new pair, but the erratic morphing seemed to have stopped and her body wasn't giving out on her.

"Ms. Clark tells me you have a good chance of winning. And that's why we're here, Ms. Mack. To win." The CEO paused. "And raise money for the Special Olympics, of course. Are you listening?"

"Uh—yes. I am."

"Good. You're part of the team—my team. We're all counting on you."

Alex didn't dare leave the school now. The CEO would notice and wonder why someone with a good chance of winning had chickened out. Every explanation Alex could think of would seem like a lame and suspicious excuse. Danielle Atron might even take Alex's absence, following her pep talk, as a personal insult. Alex couldn't afford to draw the CEO's attention for any reason.

"I'm waiting," Ms. Atron said impatiently. "Anxiously."

"Just one more minute," Alex stuffed her old clothes into her backpack and found her brush and ponytail holder. "I'm almost ready."

Alex secured her hair into a ponytail with the holder. That didn't completely control the fly-away effect, but it helped. Gripping the toilet seat, Alex unlocked the door with her foot. Then, slinging her backpack over her shoulder, she walked out.

Danielle Atron was waiting for her by the locker room door. As usual, she was impeccably dressed today in a light green linen suit with a cream-colored blouse. Not a strand of her short, dark hair was out of place.

Alex hesitated. She couldn't touch the metal handle on the locker room door, but clearly the CEO was expecting Alex to open the door for her.

"Any time, Ms. Mack," Ms. Atron said impatiently.

Alex walked toward her, forcing a smile. "After you."

"Out." The CEO opened the door and stood back to let Alex pass.

"Thank you." As she walked by, Alex saw wisps of Ms. Atron's hair stand on end. A puzzled frown darkened the woman's face as the linen suit plastered itself to her arms and legs. Before the door closed, Alex saw the CEO take a mini-recorder from her purse and heard her mutter into it, "Monday. Locate new dry cleaner. Sue the old one for cruel and unusual inconvenience."

Spotting a pay phone by the entrance, Alex stopped and fished a quarter out of her backpack. Annie didn't know about the electrical havoc her helmet had created in Alex's system. But maybe if Alex only held the plastic receiver and used a pencil to push the buttons, she'd be all right.

I hope, Alex thought desperately as she listened

to the ringing, *she'll know what to do about it.* The answering machine picked up, and Alex banged the receiver down with a frustrated groan. Annie and her parents were already at the school or on their way. Alex hurried outside.

The parade of athletes was in progress on the field. Robyn and Raymond marched with the rest of the team. Jackie and Nicole had linked arms and were waving. Kelly walked up front by Scott, who was carrying the school banner. The flags from the five competing schools were flying from the top of the stands, and the stadium was packed with cheering friends and families.

Alex shook off a twinge of regret for not being out there with the team. But then she remembered that the event was a tribute to the real Olympics and everything they stood for, especially sportsmanship. Alex could not betray the ancient traditions and spirit of the games by competing dishonestly. The thought made her feel a little better.

Vince stepped into view and Alex ducked under the bleachers. She moved slowly toward the far end, being careful not to touch the support struts. Pausing in the shadows under the stands, she picked more bits of debris off her shorts and shoes before moving out onto the path by the bleachers.

"Yo, Alex!" Louis saw her as he walked by. He was holding a bunch of school pennants. "Why are you under the bleachers instead of marching in the parade?" he asked.

Alex faltered. "I—uh—I'm late and I was hoping no one would notice." Trying to appear casual, Alex said, "I thought you were on vacation."

"Got back last night. Ray talked me into selling these flags." Louis shrugged. "It's for a good cause, I guess. Wanna buy one?"

"Maybe later, if you have any left." Alex saw that the tips of the felt triangles were all pointing in her direction.

"I'll save one for you. Good luck today."

Louis moved on, and Alex cautiously peeked out. Gymnastics equipment and blue tumbling mats filled the area inside the track. Metal benches had been placed in front of the bleachers for the teams and their coaches. Dave was setting up a large sun shade in front of the Danielle Atron Junior High bleachers. As the athletes ran off the field after the parade was finished, Nicole spotted Alex and ran over.

"Feeling better?" Nicole was not affected by

the flyaway effect because her braided black hair was tightly tucked and pinned and she was wearing a snug leotard.

"A lot better," Alex said. "Guess I just panicked."

"I'm feeling a little panicked myself right now." Nicole smiled. "The only good thing about doing my routine early is that I can relax for the rest of the day when I'm done—win or lose."

Alex grinned. "You'll do great."

"Nicole!" Raymond yelled. "Mr. Hokaido wants you!"

"Gotta go," Nicole said. "Catch ya later."

As Nicole ran off, Raymond spotted Alex and stomped over.

"Where have you been, Alex?" Raymond demanded, looking annoyed. "Everyone else got here on time."

"Please, don't come too close!" Holding out her hand, Alex shrank back. "Have you seen Annie?"

"No." Puzzled, Raymond stopped. "Your mom is by the judges' stand with the video crew and your dad is in the bleachers, but I haven't seen Annie. Why?"

Raymond's attitude quickly shifted from a

very serious student coach to a very worried best friend as Alex explained her situation.

"How are you going to run?" Raymond asked.

"Well, actually, I wasn't planning to run anyway. Using my powers to make the team wasn't right, Ray, and competing today wouldn't be either. I'm going to fake a slight injury so Jackie has to take my place. I expect you to back me up. It's only fair."

"But Alex, you've worked so hard getting in shape—just as hard as the rest of the kids. You could win."

"Winning isn't everything, you know. Besides, I've got worse problems right now. I can't even leave the grounds because Danielle Atron's taken a special interest in me." Sighing, Alex shook her head.

"Okay. Let me think." Rubbing his chin, Raymond stared at the ground. "Somehow we've got to keep you away from everyone without it being too obvious—"

"Hey! Alvaraz!" Vince shouted.

Alex felt the blood drain from her face as the plant security man headed toward them.

"That's Alvarado," Raymond said. "Raymond Al-va-ra-do."

"Whatever." Vince dismissed the correction

with an impatient wave. "I want you to go to Ms. Atron's car and get the two director's chairs from the trunk. Tell the chauffeur I sent you."

"I can't leave!" Raymond said indignantly. "The meet's going to start and I've got a team to coach."

"I'll go." Alex stepped out of the shadows.

Vince shifted his cold gaze from Raymond to Alex and back. "I don't care who goes. I just want the chair before Ms. Atron returns."

"No problem." Raymond waited until Vince was out of earshot, then whispered to Alex, "Are you nuts?"

"No. Director's chair are made of wood, so they won't make me zap. I'll ask the driver to open the trunk. And running Vince's errand gives me a good reason not to be here with the team. I've got to avoid them any way I can. Maybe Annie will show up while I'm gone."

Raymond brightened. "And if she doesn't, I'll think of something else to keep you moving until she does."

"Ray!" Robyn shouted. "Come on! Richie is first up on the parallel bars."

Stashing her backpack, Alex retraced her steps under the stands and skirted the crowd to reach the parking lot. She returned with the chairs fifteen minutes later and gave them to Raymond to give to Vince. Raymond then told her to bring out some towels from the gym.

"Hey Alex!" Mr. Mack called down to her from the stands as she headed into the school to get more towels.

"Hi, Dad!" Alex waved. "Is Annie with you?"

"She had to return some library books, but she'll be here in time for lunch. We brought a picnic basket."

"Great!" Promising to meet her parents at noon, Alex hurried into the empty school, then slowed down. Raymond didn't really need towels, he was just keeping her busy so she could avoid everybody. Everybody except Annie that is. *Why can't she be here when I really need her?* Alex wondered.

Alex managed to keep moving all morning. When it was Nicole's turn on the balance beam, she watched from under the stands and cheered when Nicole placed second. On her second trip to the refreshment booth to get lemonade for the team, she watched Nicole perform her floor exercises. Nicole came in third. Alex hurried off with the drinks as Dave walked up and ordered two hot dogs and fries. Like everyone else who worked at Paradise Valley Chemical, he had shown up to support the CEO's project. He was not looking for the GC-161 kid today.

When the gymnastics events were over, Danielle Atron Junior High was in second place behind Greenfield by two points. Trailing the leading schools by ten points, Peaceful View and Lancaster were tied for third. Unless something went drastically wrong in the track events, it would be a fight to the finish between Atron and Greenfield.

Waiting under the stands for Raymond as the crowd dispersed for lunch, Alex removed more trash from her shoes and socks. So far everyone had been too busy or nervous or excited to notice that she attracted litter like a magnet and hadn't stopped moving for hours.

"Any sign of Annie?" Raymond asked when he joined her.

Alex shook her head. Annie didn't know there was a problem, and if she didn't arrive soon, Alex was in big trouble. The broad jump was scheduled to begin immediately following lunch. Alex had to show up at the bench with the rest of the team and fake her injury right before the event started. Timing was crucial. Jackie might freak if she had too much time to think about actually competing. If Alex wasn't un-electrified before the team assembled, the static-electrical havoc she created would make too many people ask too many questions.

Raymond and Alex took the long way around the field to the gate. Alex's parents had settled under a large tree on the campus lawn.

"Hey, kids!" Mr. Mack grinned. "Hope you're hungry."

"Famished," Raymond said.

"Me, too." Alex sat on the edge of the blanket opposite her father and mother. Strands of Mrs. Mack's blond hair reached toward Alex. Her mother casually brushed them back.

"I'm not surprised." Mrs. Mack set paper plates and napkins in front of them, then dumped a handful of silverware in front of Mr. Mack. "You didn't stop running all morning, Alex. I bet I've got shots of you dashing back and forth in half the video footage we've taken so far."

Raymond grabbed his plate and napkin as they moved toward Alex, while she slapped her hand over hers to hold them down. Mr. Mack's eyes were closed as he strained to open a jar of pickles. Mrs. Mack lifted a plastic tub of cold cuts and cheese out of the basket. Neither one had noticed.

"You'll be worn out before you get a chance to race, Alex." The pickle jar lid popped. Mr. Mack put the open jar down and stuck a fork inside. "Or were you just warming up?"

"Just warming up."

"And helping me." Raymond stabbed a pickle and held the fork out to Alex.

Starved, Alex took it without thinking. A bolt of electrical energy shot from her fingers and into the metal utensil. Her mouth fell open as fork and pickle rocketed upward into the tree.

CHAPTER 12

The prongs of the fork, with pickle intact, lodged in a branch above Alex. At the same moment, her right hand turned into silvery ooze, and she gasped and tucked it behind her.

"Didn't you bring the hot mustard?" Mr. Mack asked, looking over Mrs. Mack's shoulder into the basket.

"The mustard is in here somewhere, George." Mrs. Mack handed him a bowl of potato salad. "There it is."

Alex looked up at the branch and, without meaning to, unleashed a telekinetic surge. It zapped the fork and wrenched it free with a *twang*. Her heart stood still as she saw the fork and pickle descending.

Raymond caught the fork as it dropped. He blinked with surprise, then brushed bits of bark off the pickle. After examining the pickle closely, he shrugged and took a bite.

Heaving a weary sigh, Alex sagged with relief. Her parents hadn't noticed a thing.

"Mmmm, crisp and juicy," Raymond said. "Why don't you have a pickle, Alex?"

"I think I'll pass on the pickles," Alex said.

"There's Annie." Mr. Mack pointed across the lawn and whistled. "Over here, Annie!"

Finally! Spotting Annie running toward them, Alex started to stand up, then realized she had jelly feet. She waited on hands and knees, hoping her powers wouldn't betray her.

"Did I miss anything?" Annie held her hand out for a chip as Mr. Mack tugged open the bag.

"Nothing important," he said. The bag ripped from seam to seam and a cascade of chips fell into Mr. Mack's lap. He gave one to Annie and said, "Alex doesn't race until this afternoon."

Feeling her feet solidify, Alex jumped forward and grabbed Annie's arm. "We have to talk," Alex said in a quiet but urgent tone. Annie's shoulder-length hair sprang to attention and her blouse crackled. "Now," Alex added.

"Is there a problem?" Annie asked carefully.

"Yes. It's electrifying!" Alex stared hard at Annie, hoping she'd get the hint.

Suddenly realizing her clothes were hugging her skin, Annie folded her arms across her chest and announced, "We'll be right back."

As they started across the lawn, Alex looked over her shoulder and motioned to Raymond to follow.

"Where are they going in such a hurry?" Mr. Mack asked.

"Got me." Raymond quickly slapped a sandwich together and stood up. "I've gotta go, too. Thanks for the sandwich."

As Raymond caught up, Alex launched into a hurried explanation of what had gone on that morning. "Annie, tell me you know what's happening to me. Please," Alex finished.

"The helmet got switched to rheostat and you fell asleep with your hand on the phone charge-nodes," Annie explained. "Your body soaked up electrical energy through the electrodes for over three hours." Annie lowered her gaze sheepishly. "I honestly didn't know there was anything terribly wrong, Alex."

"Neither did I until I got here and all the kids started laughing at me," Alex said. "So what do we do about it, Annie?"

"We have to get rid of the excess energy," Annie said. "That's what your body's trying to do every time you touch something metal, but the discharges are too powerful for doors and metal bars to absorb. We need something big— and grounded." Annie stopped and scanned the area around the school.

"Like what?" Raymond asked.

"Like that." Annie pointed to a row of telephone poles on a rise beyond the stadium.

"Power lines?" Alex paled. "I'm not touching any power lines. I'll electrocute myself. I'm not *that* desperate!"

"Or that stupid," Raymond added.

"Of course not." Annie sighed patiently. "But the ground wire is perfectly safe, and it's designed to handle excessive and sudden infusions of electricity. It drains extra energy harmlessly into the ground. Dirt isn't a conductor."

By the time the three of them reached the top of the incline, spectators and participants were beginning to wander back into the stadium below for the afternoon session.

"Over here." Annie moved to a grounded pole. A heavy cable stretched from the high crossbeam to the ground, and the scrub bushes growing around it provided some cover. "Okay,

Alex. I want you to imagine that your elbow is a resistor."

"What's a resistor?" Alex asked.

"It's like—a dam. Pretend your elbow is a kink in a wire that will only allow a small stream of energy to pass through. You've got to try and regulate the flow instead of dumping all the energy at once. We don't want to overdo it. Okay?"

Alex nodded.

"Whenever you're ready."

Closing her eyes, Alex pictured a dam and grabbed the ground wire. Immediately she felt a powerful surge through her body and tried to control it. But the force of the electrical energy rushing out of her was so great, it smashed into the imagined dam and blew it apart.

So much for regulating the flow, Alex thought as a raging river of electricity poured out of her and into the ground wire. She trembled as the excess energy coursed through her arm. Hot flashes danced from one part of her body to another as she morphed and unmorphed in rapid, erratic bursts. A tremendous telekinetic tension built in her mind, but she couldn't stop the monster surge from escaping. She opened her eyes when Annie yelled, "Duck!"

Annie and Raymond hit the dirt, flinging their

arms over their heads. Every loose twig, leaf, and paper on the ground around them was swept into the telekinetic tornado Alex had created. The whirling dust devil zoomed toward them.

Concentrating her hardest, Alex launched a second telekinetic command at the ministorm. The funnel swerved, barely missing Annie and Raymond as it tore down the hill and across a vacant lot, sucking dirt and rocks and brush into it as it went. It lost speed and disappeared before it reached the road.

Still the electrical energy poured out of Alex. Unharmed, but worried, she looked at Annie and Raymond.

They slowly raised their heads, then glanced at the power lines above.

"Uh-oh." Raymond's eyes widened.

"Oops," Annie said.

Alex looked up and choked back a cry. Streaks of purple and yellow lightning sped along the wires toward the school. The wires cracked and sparked and flashed, leaving the three of them gaping in amazement.

A moment later, chaos hit the stadium.

The power and electrical current flowing out of Alex decreased suddenly. Letting go of the ground wire, she dropped down beside Raymond and Annie. At that moment the massive concentration of energy entered the school's electrical system.

Alex watched in silent awe.

The marching band music playing through the PA system blared at full volume, then sped up.

The bulbs in the overhead stadium lights exploded in a shower of sparks and loud cracks.

The numbers on the digital scoreboard flashed in different colors and changed at split-second intervals.

Bells clanged inside the school.

Everyone in the stadium covered their ears and paused to gaze at the spectacle.

"What happened?" Raymond asked as the startling effects of the electrical overload subsided.

"The dam broke," Alex muttered. She winced as a single, surviving lightbulb shattered.

"And the ground cable couldn't process that much energy all at once," Annie added. "The overflow had no place to go but into the power lines." Annie turned to Alex. "Are you all right?"

"I think so." Alex sat up. Bits of grass and leaves that hadn't been captured by the telekinetic tornado fell off her clothes. Grinning, she picked a leaf out of Annie's hair. It was a tangled mess, but the flyaway effect was gone. So was the super-static electrical field Alex had been engulfed in.

"Are we in trouble?" Raymond asked, still watching the stadium. People scratched their heads and milled about in confusion, but no one seemed to be hurt.

"Except for the lightbulbs, no real harm was done," Annie said. "We're certainly not going to confess. Who'd believe it anyhow?"

In the stadium, Mr. Hokaido, Ms. Clark, and several other coaches were walking the track to make sure it was clear of splintered glass. The team was filing in through the gate.

"We have to get moving, Ray. It's going to take a while to get back without being seen." Alex headed down the rise.

They circled the school and raced through the parking lot. The high school principal was talking to a power company employee who had been called to investigate the huge power surge. As Annie suspected, there had been no damage except shattered lightbulbs.

The rest of the team was already on the bench, listening to an impassioned speech by Vince. Danielle Atron sat in her chair under the sun shade. Her gaze followed Alex as she and Raymond squeezed onto the end of the bench.

"Think victory!" Vince proclaimed, standing with his legs apart and his knuckles on his hips. He reminded Alex of the drill sergeants she had seen in movies. "Nothing less than winning the school trophy will be tolerated. Do you understand me?"

"Yes," the team mumbled.

"I can't hear you!" Vince barked.

"Victory!" Ellen shouted above the other athletes.

Most of the team picked up the chant. Alex noticed Mr. Hokaido and Ms. Clark exchange disturbed glances. She watched for the others' response to Vince. Raymond sighed. Scott frowned. Nicole rolled her eyes. Jackie looked over her shoulder and smiled at a tanned, athletic looking man who blew her a kiss. *Must be Jackie's father*, Alex thought.

Alex's heart jumped when someone tapped her on the shoulder. It was Robyn, standing behind the bench.

"You're fifth in the broad jump, Alex."

"Thanks." Smiling tightly, Alex braced herself as Ms. Clark waved her onto the field. She nudged Raymond, sitting beside her. "On the count of three, stand up and bump into me. One. Two. Three."

Alex and Raymond stood up. Pretending to lose his balance, Raymond fell against her. Alex stumbled and, grabbing the bench, fell to her knees. Raymond acted totally surprised as he helped her up. Alex took a hobbling step, with Raymond holding her by the elbow.

Robyn gasped.

Jackie jumped to her feet and stared.

Ms. Clark was at Alex's side in a second. "How bad is it?"

"It hurts, but I don't think it's sprained or anything." Alex bit her lower lip as she tried to walk.

"Man, I'm sorry, Alex," Raymond said with convincing dismay.

"Don't worry about it, Ray." *You're doing just fine,* she added silently. *Everything is going according to plan.* Sighing dramatically, Alex winced for Ms. Riley's benefit, and then said, "Jackie can jump instead."

"Me?" Jackie's face went white. "You want me to jump?"

"That's what alternates are for." Ms. Clark pointed to the bench and said, "Sit down, Alex. Make sure she doesn't move, Robyn. And, Raymond, get the nurse from the first-aid station. Jackie, come with me. You're on."

Alex glanced back at Danielle Atron, sitting in her chair. She was frowning as Vince whispered in her ear. Nodding, Ms. Atron turned her attention to Jackie.

In the stands, Mr. Addison looked almost as pale as his daughter. But when Jackie looked up at him, he gave her an encouraging smile.

"Too bad about your ankle, Alex." Nicole sat down beside her and offered her a sip of lemonade.

"It's not serious," Alex said. Alex hated lying to her friend, but there was no way out of it. "Congratulations on winning your medals," Alex added.

Nicole fingered the bronze and silver medals around her neck and smiled. "They are kind of cool, huh? When I look at them, I think about all the Special Olympics kids we've helped today. Just imagine how winning a medal must feel to them."

"Must feel great. I hope Jackie wins, too," Alex said. She really meant it. Jackie would be thrilled to perform well.

Jackie took her position behind the starting line. Alex held her breath as Jackie crouched and then ran. It was a great jump. Silence reigned as the officials measured the distance, then called out the results. Jackie was in the lead by six inches.

Whooping with the rest of the team, Alex jumped to her feet and applauded just as Raymond arrived with the nurse. Realizing her mistake, Alex quickly sat back down.

Eyeing Alex sternly, the nurse checked her ankle, then handed Robyn a paper giving Alex permission to compete. Slipping it into her clipboard, Robyn left to assemble the boys entered in pole vaulting. The nurse headed directly for Ms. Clark, near the broad jump.

"Now what?" Raymond asked. "Ms. Clark is going to think you're faking."

Alex shrugged. "I'll think of something." She had to, for Jackie.

None of the remaining girls came close to topping Jackie's distance. A warm rush of satisfaction flooded Alex as Jackie stepped onto the top riser to accept her gold medal. Tears of joy rolled down the girl's face as she caught her father's eye. Mr. Addison cheered and smiled proudly.

On the sidelines, Alex saw the nurse take Ms. Clark aside. The coach frowned, then nodded and sighed.

"I can't believe I won." Laughing, Jackie bounced with excitement as she returned to the bench.

"You've got a gold medal to prove it." Nicole grinned and winked at Alex. "We knew you could do it."

"Never had a doubt," Alex agreed.

Jackie's grin faded. "This should have been yours, Alex. If you hadn't hurt yourself—"

"Alex, can I see you for a minute?" Ms. Clark asked.

"Sure." Alex followed Ms. Clark to a secluded area by the stands. The coach was obviously upset.

"Alex, the nurse just told me that there's nothing wrong with your ankle. She says you're in good enough condition to compete. You've let yourself and the team down by quitting. I can't even begin to tell you how disappointed I am."

Alex felt as if she had been punched in the stomach. "I'm not a quitter, Ms. Clark."

"Did you fake twisting your ankle?" The coach looked her directly in the eye, demanding an honest answer.

"Yes, but not because I was afraid." Alex sagged. "I didn't deserve to be on the team in the first place, and Jackie did."

"How do you figure that?" Ms. Clark was obviously mystified.

"If Jackie hadn't turned her ankle at the try-outs, she would have beaten me easily. My performance was just a fluke. Jackie *has* to run instead of me, Ms. Clark. Winning the school trophy is just too important to the team and you and Mr. Hokaido—"

Alex stopped herself before she said too much. Raymond had overheard Danielle Atron threaten to fire the coaches if the team didn't win, but nobody was supposed to know that.

Ms. Clark frowned. "You've trained so hard, Alex. You've earned the right to compete, and you have just as great a chance of winning as Jackie does."

"I can't explain why, Ms. Clark, but it wouldn't be fair. It's the Olympics. It's a matter of honor. Let Jackie run."

"I don't understand, but if that's what you want—"

"It's the right thing to do." Alex sighed as Ms. Clark nodded and left. Now Ms. Clark and the team thought she was a quitter. That hadn't been part of the plan.

CHAPTER 13

Alex took a few minutes to find her parents and explain that she had gotten sick to her stomach. She didn't want to fake a limp at home for the next few days and she couldn't tell them the truth, either. Annie understood and supported her story by saying that she too had had nausea the night before. Mr. and Mrs. Mack were disappointed, but assured Alex that a length of ribbon and a piece of metal weren't as important as her health.

Now that she didn't have to worry about giving her friends frizzy hair or clinging clothes, Alex could sit with the team. But she felt even more removed from her teammates, except for her close friends, than she had that morning.

Some of the kids had overheard the nurse tell Ms. Clark that Alex was able to compete, so she couldn't explain why Jackie was taking her place. The rumor that she had chickened out and quit spread quickly.

"Too bad about your ankle, Alex." Kelly grinned as she passed by. She was wearing a gold medal for winning ninth-grade gymnastics. "And don't let what the other kids are saying bother you. Lots of people buckle under the stress of competition."

"Sure they do." Ellen blew on her silver medal and polished it on her shirt.

Cheeks flaming, Alex suffered the taunts in silence. She knew she was acting honorably, and so did Raymond. Robyn, Nicole, and Jackie assumed she had her reasons for dropping out of the meet and didn't press her.

"I'm so nervous." Jackie jogged in place, getting ready for the sprint, which was the next event. "But my dad says that's normal."

"He's right," Raymond said. "Being nervous gives you that winning edge. Don't worry about the other runners. Just keep your eyes on the track. Let's go!" Raymond jogged off with Jackie beside him.

Alex and Nicole stood up as the race started.

A Greenfield runner took an early lead, but Alex could tell that Jackie was pacing herself. Then, as Jackie moved up on the leader, the girl in the next lane stumbled and brushed Jackie with her elbow. The referee didn't call the accidental infraction. Although Jackie didn't break stride, the interference affected her timing. She finished a close second.

"That was a tough break," Nicole said as Jackie came off the track. "You ran a great race."

"That's five more points for the team and now you've got a silver medal, too," Alex added enthusiastically.

Jackie went on to win a bronze on the hurdle course, and Alex could see she was thrilled to be taking home three medals.

During the fifteen-minute break before the final event, the coaches rallied the team. Mr. Hokaido reported that none of the other schools were close to Greenfield and Danielle Atron Junior High in points. If Atron Junior High won the relay, they would win the trophy. Then Ms. Clark stepped forward.

"One member of this team voluntarily forfeited her chance to win a medal for the good of the team." The coach paused to smile at Alex.

Alex shifted uncomfortably as everyone

turned to stare. *Now would not be a good time to start glowing*, Alex told herself.

Ms. Clark continued. "She said it was because this is the Olympics, and because honor and fairness are far more important than winning. That's one of the reasons Mr. Hokaido and I would like the alternates, including Alex Mack, to run the relay race."

Danielle Atron stiffened in her chair and glared at the coaches. Alex stared at Ms. Clark and Mr. Hokaido. If the alternates ran and lost, Danielle Atron would make sure the coaches lost their jobs.

"But we've all worked so hard," Ellen whined. "And we're so close to winning the school trophy."

"The alternates have worked just as hard as the rest of you," Ms. Clark said. "They came to every practice knowing they probably wouldn't compete. That kind of effort and dedication deserves a chance."

"Besides, the kids on the other teams are tired after competing all day," Mr. Hokaido added. "We have great athletes on our alternate team, and they're fresh."

"That's right. They're not worn out because they haven't done anything all day." Nicole nodded thoughtfully. "That just might give them the winning edge."

Alex listened in a daze. There were a boy and a girl track alternate for each grade. Six kids including her. The school trophy would go to the winner of the six-person relay race.

Raymond stood up. "Jackie was an alternate, and she got a first, second, and third. Our alternates are great athletes, and I think they should be allowed to compete."

Mr. Hokaido put it to a vote. "All those in favor of letting the alternates run the relay, raise your hands."

Everyone raised their hands.

The next thing Alex knew, Raymond was hustling her into the proper lane on the track. Other runners waited in their lanes on either side of her. She was in the number six position, the last to run. If the race was close, it would be up to her to win it.

"Just do your best, Alex," Raymond said.

"What if my best isn't good enough?" Alex asked nervously.

"It'll be good enough for me. So quit worrying and burn some sneaker rubber." Giving her hand a quick squeeze, Raymond dashed off the track.

Taking a deep breath, Alex shook her arms and legs to limber up. Ahead of her, the number one runners gripped their batons and crouched to start. The gun went off.

The Danielle Atron runner was in third place, behind runners from two other schools, at the first hand-off. That boy was still running third when he handed off to runner number three, but he had gained a little. Darleen Higgins lost ground but maintained third place as she passed the baton to runner number four. Number four passed the second-place runner just before he handed off to Roger Thomas, in the fifth position.

Greenfield was still in the lead as the number five runners pounded around the curve.

Alex wiped her hands on her shorts, wondering how she was going to hold on to the baton with sweaty palms. Dropping it would disqualify the team. She glanced at the Greenfield girl in the lane to her right. The girl glared at her a moment, then turned her attention to the track.

As the number five runners raced toward her, Alex braced herself. They were only a few feet behind now.

I can do this, Alex told herself as she flexed her fingers. *I have to do this.*

The baton was in her hand and she was off.

Alex ran as though Vince were on her heels. Her feet pounded the track. She listened to the rhythm and sped up the pace. Faster. Faster. Her legs surged with the power of muscles honed to fitness through hard work. The gap between her and the Greenfield girl began to close.

Willing her legs to move still faster, Alex drew even with the Greenfield leader. They raced neck and neck for the finish-line ribbon across the track ahead. The roar of the crowd was a distant thunder in Alex's ears. Then she heard her name.

"Go Alex! Go Alex!"

With a burst of speed generated by sheer will power, Alex broke through the ribbon.

Gasping for breath, she stumbled to a halt. Raymond reached her first and grabbed her by the arms. "You did it! You did it! I knew you could do it. We won!"

"We did?" Taking big gulps of air, Alex blinked. "I won?"

"You won, fair and square," Raymond said. Alex grinned at him as the truth sank in. She had won the race without using any of her extraordinary powers. She had won through hard work, practice, and discipline. And that was a powerful feeling.

A moment later the alternates were surrounded by their cheering teammates. Swept along in the excited crush, Alex glimpsed Ms. Clark out of the corner of her eye. The coach smiled and gave her a thumbs up.

High in the stands, Alex saw her dad jump up and down and wave frantically. She waved back, giggling. He nudged the man beside him, pointed at her, then at himself. Alex could almost hear him saying, "That's my daughter." Annie just nodded and grinned.

Standing at the finish line with the video crew, her mother wiped away tears. Then she dashed onto the track and gave Alex a huge hug. "I'm so proud of you, Alex!"

"Thanks, Mom." Alex felt her own eyes mist. Her family's loving pride was worth more than any award.

Alex spent the next half hour in a delirious daze of joy. All the runners on the relay team were awarded gold medals. Then all the teams returned to their benches for the school trophy presentation.

Danielle Atron and Vince joined the officials on the field. As founder and sole financial sponsor of the event, the CEO had given herself the honor of presenting the large, gleaming trophy.

Kelly graciously accepted it for Danielle Atron Junior High. Ms. Atron was obviously delighted to give it to her namesake school.

Vince announced that pizza and drinks for the winning team and their families would be served on the campus after pictures were taken.

As everyone moved back to the risers for the photo session, Danielle Atron and Vince passed Alex without giving her a second glance. A wave of relief washed over her. Now that the trophy had been won, the CEO no longer had any interest in her.

"Okay, Vince," Ms. Atron was saying. "We had an Olympics and we won an Olympics, but the fun and games are over now. You still haven't found that kid."

"I'm working on it." Vince sighed. "I'm working on it."

Dave tugged on Vince's sleeve. "Can I stay for pizza, too?"

Alex smiled. Everything was back to normal.

"Hurry up, Alex!" Nicole waved her over to the group gathered on the risers. All her friends were sitting on the ground in the front row. "They won't let us eat until after the pictures are taken."

"There's a price for everything," Robyn said as she edged over to make room for Alex.

"And I'm starving." Raymond frowned.

"You're always starving." Louis handed Alex an Olympic pennant. "It's on me. You did great."

"We all did great," Jackie said.

"Yes." Raymond grinned. "Everyone's a winner today."

Alex nodded and touched the gold medal hanging around her neck. Being a winner was a wonderful feeling, but gold medals weren't worth anything unless they were won honestly, through hard work and fair play.

"Ready everyone?" The photographer held up his hand. "Say cheese."

The team shouted in unison, "Pizza!"

About the Author

Diana G. Gallagher lives in Kansas with her husband, Marty Burke, two dogs, three cats, and a cranky parrot. When she's not writing, she likes to read and take long walks with the dogs.

A Hugo Award–winning illustrator, she is best known for her series *Woof: The House Dragon*. Her songs about humanity's future are sung throughout the world and have been recorded in cassette form: "Cosmic Concepts More Complete," "Star*Song," and "Fire Dream." Diana and Marty, an Irish folksinger, perform traditional and original music at science-fiction conventions as a duo.

Her first adult novel, *The Alien Dark*, appeared in 1990. She is also the author of a *Star Trek: Deep Space Nine*® novel for young readers, *Arcade*, and four other books in *The Secret World of Alex Mack* series, all available from Minstrel Books.

She is currently working on another *Star Trek* novel and a new *Alex Mack* story.